2002

D0389412

a thousand rooms
— of —
dream and fear

a
thousand rooms
of
dream and fear

◆ ◆ ◆ ◆ ◆ ◆ ◆

A NOVEL

◆ ◆ ◆ ◆ ◆

atiq rahimi

TRANSLATED FROM DARI BY
SARAH MAGUIRE AND YAMA YARI

OTHER PRESS • NEW YORK

Other Press edition 2011

The publisher is grateful to the Arts Council England for a grant toward the translation of this book.

Production Editor: *Yvonne E. Cárdenas*
Book design: *Simon M. Sullivan*
This book was set in 10.5 pt Galliard by Alpha Design & Composition of Pittsfield, NH.

10 9 8 7 6 5 4 3 2 1

LIBRARY OF CONGRESS CATALOGING-IN-PUBLICATION DATA

Rahimi, Atiq.
[Hazār khānah-i khvāb va ikhtināq. English]
A thousand rooms of dream and fear / Atiq Rahimi ; translated from Dari by Sarah Maguire and Yama Yari.
p. cm.
ISBN 978-1-59051-361-3 — ISBN 978-1-59051-362-0 (e-book)
I. Maguire, Sarah, 1957- II. Yari, Yama, 1980- III. Title.
PK6878.9.R34H3913 2011
891'.543—dc22

2010038973

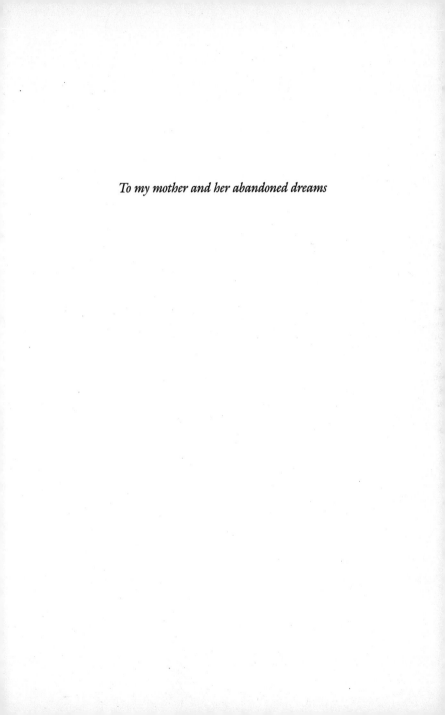

To my mother and her abandoned dreams

Unless sleep is less restless than wakefulness, do not rest!

SHAMS-E TABRIZI

a thousand rooms
— of —
dream and fear

"Father?"

"Fuck your father!"

Have I got my eyes shut or is it dark? I can't tell. Maybe it's night and I'm dreaming. But then why would I be thinking like this?

No, I am awake, but my eyes are closed. I'm sure I've been asleep. I remember having a dream where a child cried out, "Father."

What child? I've got no idea. I didn't recognize his voice. Maybe it was me when I was a child, looking for my father.

"Father!"

The same voice! So it wasn't a dream. The voice seems to be coming from somewhere above my head. I must open my eyes.

"Who are you?"

Trying to speak is absolute agony. A violent pain shoots right through my temples. Darkness descends. Then total silence.

What has happened to that child? His voice is shaking with fear, and his breath is foul. It's as though he's calling to me from a cesspit or from the bottom of a dried-up well.

"Father!"

It sounds like he's fallen down a well and he's trying to get his father to save him . . . But what well? Aren't I at home? I must be at home. I'm home in bed, asleep. I'm asleep and I'm thirsty, so I've had this dream about a dried-up well.

"Father?"

But no, that voice isn't coming from the bottom of a well. I can't possibly be dreaming. That voice is coming from directly above my head.

I can actually feel it. I can feel its vibrations. I can feel the hot, anxious breath spilling its words on my frozen skin.

But why can't I see him?

"Father!"

"Be quiet! Go inside!"

And now whose is that other voice? Is it my mother?

"Mother!"

My own voice chokes in my throat. I am still in a dream. Not a dream, a nightmare. A nightmare where you scream but can't make a sound. A nightmare where you think you're awake but you're unable to open your eyes or move a muscle. Where you're completely paralyzed.

My grandfather used to say that, according to Da Mullah Saed Mustafa, when you're asleep your soul leaves your body and wanders around. And if you wake up before your soul has come back to your body, you get trapped in a terrible nightmare where you're paralyzed and totally powerless. Struck dumb. Petrified, abandoned. And you stay like that till your soul returns. My grandfather used to say that my grandmother had a heart attack because she tried to get up before her soul returned to her body.

I mustn't get up! I have to stay here in bed till my soul comes back. I mustn't open my eyes. I mustn't allow myself to think about anything other than this. The only thing you're supposed to do in bed is say your prayers. It's forbidden to think about anything else. In bed, Satan can take over your thoughts. That's what Da Mullah Saed Mustafa told grandfather, and grandfather told me. I will stop thinking. I'll do nothing but say the Kalima till my soul comes back home. In the Name of Allah . . .

I've collapsed. I've been kicked into a ditch by two jack-booted men.

They've cursed and sworn at me.

"Fuck your father!"

Before falling asleep, I must cross my arms over my heart and recite one of the ninety-nine names of God one hundred and one times. Al-Ba'ith, one. Al-Ba'ith, two. Al-Ba'ith, three . . . My grandfather used to say that Da Mullah Saed Mustafa told him that by reciting the ninety-nine names you can tame all the creatures in a nightmare. Al-Ba'ith, four. Al-Ba'ith, five. Al-Ba'ith, six . . .

I can smell stale shit and fresh blood.

"Father!"

But how can I possibly be having a nightmare? That child's voice is as real as the stench of shit and blood.

"Who are you?"

But the words die in my throat. I'm too weak to think straight. I must open my eyes . . . but I can't see a thing.

Darkness . . . nothing but darkness.

No, I can't be asleep. I've been taken over by the forces of darkness. The djinn have come, they are squatting on my chest. My grandfather used to say that, according to Da Mullah Saed Mustafa—who was more important than ten Mullahs put together—the djinn live in those rooms that don't have a Koran. And when you're asleep at night and your soul has gone wandering about, they come and take over your body. They sit on your chest. They pin down your arms. They blindfold your eyes. They gag your mouth. Then they insult you and curse your family. But you must ignore them completely. Otherwise they'll have got you forever. Your only hope is to say your prayers. Call out the name of God! If you don't pray, the djinn will stay squatting on your chest, and your soul will never come back.

"Brother!"

That's not my mother. It's my sister, Parwaneh.

"Parwaneh, my love, is that you? Parwaneh, little sister, please get these djinn off my chest! Parwaneh, can you hear me?"

No, she can't hear me. The djinn have imprisoned my voice in my chest.

If only she could see them!

But how could Parwaneh see the djinn? She's not important enough. My grandfather used to say that only Da Mullah Saed Mustafa could see the djinn. He was so powerful he'd even cast a spell on them and they were at his command. The djinn were his informers. Everyone had to speak well of him, even behind his back, otherwise the djinn . . . Maybe these really are Da Mullah Saed Mustafa's djinn. The djinn my grandfather said were watching us all the time at home, so we'd get found out if we were naughty. But I used to curse the djinn. At night, when I was outdoors with my cousins, we used to find a big tree in a corner of an abandoned orchard behind a ruined wall, and we used to piss there, hoping we had pissed on Da Mullah Saed Mustafa's djinn. Tonight those djinn have come back to piss on my chest.

If Parwaneh sees the djinn she'll be possessed.

"Parwaneh, little one, please go away, don't stay here!"

The djinn have stolen my voice from my throat.

The officer shot me a look of pure hatred. He bawled at me:

"The commander's going to fuck your fucking sister hard!"

Then I felt the Kalashnikov butt thud into my guts. Everything went black. Vomit shot up my throat and sprayed out all over the officer's uniform, all over his gun, all over the photo of Hafizullah Amin dangling from the mirror of the jeep . . . The jeep stopped. Two jackbooted men hauled me out. They kicked and kicked me until I fell into the sewer by the side of the road.

They swore and shouted at me:

"Fuck your father!"

"Brother!"

Parwaneh is still here by my bed.

"Parwaneh, little one, is that you? If it's you, stay and say the Kalima with me. Recite a verse from the Koran and get these djinn off my chest. Dear Parwaneh, my soul got lost in the backstreets of the city and it was captured by these two men wearing jackboots and now the djinn have taken over my body. My soul has been kicked into the sewer. My soul is hurt, dear Parwaneh, please stay with your brother, please read me the Koran . . . Cast the djinn out so my battered soul can come home to my poor damaged body. Parwaneh?"

Parwaneh is gone. She has left me. She thinks I'm asleep. She has no idea the djinn have possessed me.

It's not that long till morning prayers. And then after prayers my mother will come and sit by my bed. Gently and quietly. As always, under her breath, she will whisper a prayer by my side. Tenderly. She will protect me with her prayers. Gentler than the breeze, the djinn will melt away. My eyes will open. And instead of grumbling, I will smile at my mother. I will kiss her hands. I will prostrate myself before her. Around my neck I will wear the talisman my grandfather got from Da Mullah Saed Mustafa. I will believe in heaven and in the heavenly host of angels, I will think continuously of my soul. Every night, before I go to sleep, I will wash and then I will pray. I will not masturbate in bed. I will cross my clean hands over my heart and I will repeat the name of God a hundred and one times, Al-Ba'ith, Al-Ba'ith, Al-Ba'ith . . .

"The commander's going to fuck your fucking mother."

The officer swore at me then told the two soldiers to dump me in the jeep. I was rammed in between them. The jeep pulled off. It lurched about so much I felt sick. I reached forward and gently tapped the officer on his shoulder.

"Excuse me, Commander . . ." I asked obsequiously.

The officer jerked round in fury screaming, "The commander's going to fuck your fucking sister, you scum."

I can feel cool water trickling over my face, gently cleansing the metallic taste of my blood from my lips and my nose and my eyes, cleaning away the powerful stench of shit, the heavy blackness of this long dark night. I feel movement coming back to my body, as though the djinn have fled and my soul has finally returned. I must try to open my eyes . . . but the excruciating pain in my temple is too much. I can feel my eyeballs moving behind my eyelids. Can I move my hands? I can. Am I awake? Perhaps.

In washing away these impurities, Parwaneh has scared off the djinn. My soul has survived the blows of those two jackbooted men, it has arisen from the filth. Now, slowly but surely, it is finding its way back to my body. My sore, wounded body. This is what they call the union of the body and soul. But now my body can feel the blows my soul has taken . . .

"Brother, are you feeling any better?"

"Parwaneh?"

But my broken voice is trapped in my throat.

"Can you get up?"

No, that doesn't sound like Parwaneh.

"Who are you?"

"What?"

She can't hear me. I must take a deep breath. Scorching air burns my battered lungs. My throat is raw with pain. I must open my eyes. In agony, I force my eyelids open.

Nothing but darkness. Am I still dreaming? Al-Ba'ith . . . how many? Dream within dream! Al-Ba'ith . . . Nightmare within nightmare! Al-Ba'ith . . . Blackness within blackness! Al-Ba'ith . . .

"Get up, Father!"

The child's voice is coming closer. I can see his small head looming toward me. He smiles, then he turns to someone behind him.

"Mother, did you see? I made Father wake up!"

Is it me he's calling "Father"? I try to lift my head. But my right cheek is stuck in blood and filth.

The smell of blood merges with the stench of shit, the child's face merges with the darkness. And the darkness wins.

A child called me "Father." What a beautiful ending to a nightmare. I wish my grandfather were alive. I would go and sit beside his prayer mat, which was always spread beneath him, and I'd tell him about my nightmare. Then, from under his embroidered cushion, he'd take out the book on the interpretation of dreams that was passed on to him by Da Mullah Saed Mustafa before he died. He'd undo the rubber band wrapped round the worn cover of the book, get out his magnifying glass, and recite a verse from the Koran. Next, he'd read to himself the sections related to my dream and, having compared them with each other, offer his interpretation:

"In a dream, a child represents an enemy. An unknown child is an enemy not yet encountered. Mud and filth indicate how terrified you are of this enemy . . . and cold water is a sign of the weakness of your faith."

Then he'd take off the silver ring he always wore— engraved with one of the sacred names of Allah, "Al-Jabbar"— and he'd slip it onto one of my small fingers. He'd tell me that Da Mullah Saed Mustafa had once said that, if in the space of a single day, between sunrise and sunset, you recite this particular name of God two-thousand-two-hundred and sixty times, you'll always be protected against the wrath and mischief of your enemies and oppressors . . . Al-Jabbar, one. Al-Jabbar, two. Al-Jabbar, three . . .

"Father's saying something."

Al-Jabbar . . . what number? This strange child, this unknown enemy, won't let me recite. In fact this creature is not a child at all. It's a djinn. It's trying to stop me from counting the number of times I say Allah's name. It despises the holy name of God. Al-Jabbar, Al-Jabbar, Al-Jabbar . . . Didn't my grandfather used to say that the djinn are small, like children? Al-Jabbar . . .

"Yahya, come inside!"

Al-Jabbar. I can just make out the small djinn's body as it moves around in the dark. Al-Jabbar. It's going away. Al-Jabbar. It's going further away. Al-Jabbar. Now it's stopping. Al-Jabbar. I can see exactly where it's standing. It's standing by a door. A woman's face appears in front of my eyes. Al-Jabbar.

"Brother . . ."

Is this woman a djinn as well? Al-Jabbar. Perhaps it's a different kind of djinn. Al-Jabbar. I must lift up my head.

My head is exploding with pain. I think I'm beginning to see things a little more clearly, though I still can't move a muscle. Every single one of my bones feels as though it's broken, my veins have been severed, my brain turned to pulp, my muscles torn out . . . No, I'm not trapped in a nightmare. I've not been possessed by the djinn: I am dead.

"Name?"

"Can't you read? It's on my identity card!" I said to myself.

"Farhad," I said to the officer.

He scrutinized my face, then compared it with my ID-card photo.

"Father's name?"

"Mirdad."

"Age?"

"I was born in 1337 [1958]."

"I'm not blind. That's what it says here. I asked you how old you are."

"Let me see, I'll have to work it out because I get older every year . . ."

Silently the officer waited for me to finish my sums. Why did I start this stupid game? I have no idea. Childish arrogance. He blew cigarette smoke in my face. The sneer in his voice echoed all the way down the dark street:

"And what brings you here in the middle of the night when there's a curfew on?"

I brought my heels together sharply like a well-trained

soldier, raised my right hand to my forehead in salute, and said:

"Sir, Commander, I'm not going anywhere, sir, I'm just on my way home to my mother."

"The commander's going to fuck your mother."

I am dead. This unbelievably foul smell tells me that I'm dead. After all, is it not said that, "God made man out of dirt before He breathed life into him"?

I'm dead. I've turned back into dirt. Maybe I was shot to pieces. The fact is, I'm neither dreaming nor possessed. I've died, and now I'm going through all those experiences in Imam Ghazali's Book of the Dead.

My grandfather used to say that Da Mullah Saed Mustafa told him that—according to Imam Ghazali—at the time of death, before leaving the body, the soul flies into the heart. At this precise moment, the heavy burden of the soul crushes the chest, stifling speech and paralyzing the tongue. Like when you've been thumped hard in the chest and can't speak.

Yes, I have died and I've been buried too. I've been buried in the family vault. Perhaps, who knows, I've been buried next to my grandfather. Or perhaps next to a child and his mother. Da Mullah Saed Mustafa used to say to my grandfather that when the deceased is interred in the grave, he first meets those people buried next to him, then the relatives who died shortly before him. Who knows? Maybe my grandfather will come to see me. He will come. He's bound to come and say, "So *now* you believe everything Da Mullah Saed Mustafa said! Didn't I warn you about the terrifying black-faced angels Da Mullah Saed Mustafa said descend upon the depraved alcoholic when he dies? And the words of the angel of death who commands the deceased: 'You cursed soul, leave this body and flee to your wrathful God!'? This angel then pierces the soul with a spear that, since the beginning of time, has been tempered in fire and brimstone, making the soul skitter about like a drop of mercury. But nothing can escape the angel of death. The other angels arrive to haul the soul up to heaven. God orders them to write the sinner's name in the list of the damned. Then He sends the soul back down to earth to rejoin its corpse. After that, the two interrogating angels, Nakir and Munkar, visit the grave to question the sinner's soul: 'Tell us the name of your God? What is your religion? Who is Mohammed?' The corrupt soul replies 'I do not know' to each of these questions. So God tells his angels: 'My creature lies. Light the flames of hellfire beneath him, and prop the gates of hell wide open so that the fearsome heat will burn him!' And then the gravestone he lies beneath begins to press down on his chest so his ribs are all crushed together . . ."

"Brother, quick, get up, come inside!"

Is that the angel of death or my sister? I can feel her warm hands stroking my face. My head shakes. My legs are trembling. I'm shivering inside. With pain. With cold. With the chill of the grave, with the ice of death . . .

The angel of death—or my sister—tries to lift me up. Her hair falls into my eyes. My head is spinning violently. I can feel my soul careering about inside me. Like water reaching boiling point, it surges up my throat and shoots right out of my mouth. I topple back into the filth.

The grave is even darker than the night.

As I knelt on the ground with my hands behind my head, the soldier went through my pockets. He found my ID card and my student card. He walked back to the jeep and handed them to the man in the front seat. They exchanged a few words, and then the soldier turned and shouted, "Come here!"

My legs turned to jelly. I felt as though my knees had sunk right through the tarmac. I couldn't get up.

"Are you deaf? Get up! Come here!"

I managed to haul myself up off the ground. I even took a step toward them. But then I froze again, petrified.

"Hey! Don't you understand? Come *here*!"

The soldier bellowed at me. His voice was so loud it shook the alley walls. And me. I turned from being a rock into a trembling leaf. I must have floated through the air since that's the only way I could have found myself standing right next to the jeep. The officer sitting in the front seat was holding my documents. He shone his torch directly in my face. I screwed up my eyes against the light. But I opened them quickly at the sound of his voice.

"Name!"

I am dead. I died even before I was kicked and trampled on by men in jackboots. The gravestone crushed my ribs. My soul spewed from my mouth. The angels of death came to visit me in my grave with their blackened, twisted faces, their thick moustaches, and their heavy jackboots. Then they battered me with the butts of their Kalashnikovs.

I am dead. My next-door neighbor in the graveyard is a child who keeps on calling me.

"Father!"

I can feel his little hand smoothing my hair.

"Father, get up! This time I'm awake too. Like you!"

My grandfather used to say that Da Mullah Saed Mustafa often cited the teachings of Saed Bin Zobair who said that, when someone dies and goes to Barzakh, he sees his children who have died before him. But they are complete strangers to each other. As if the father had come from a distant universe.

I don't remember having a child.

Why does the angel of death keep pouring water on my face? Is this yet another punishment to be endured in the grave? It's never mentioned in the Book of the Dead! Maybe the angel of death is trying to keep me awake so I can experience the suffering of my soul all the more.

My eyes open. I can see the faces of the child and the angel. Behind them, there's a doorway. But there's no fire, nor any sign of hell, on the other side. Maybe this means I was never a real sinner. After all, I only drank alcohol. I never murdered anyone.

No, what you did isn't important. What's really important is what you didn't do. That was another of Da Mullah Saed Mustafa's lectures to my grandfather. You never prayed five times a day. You never made the Hajj. You never gave alms . . . You never fought jihad for God. You never became His martyr!

And all that means I'm not a true Muslim. That means I'm full of sin. Yet even so, it seems as though the angels haven't yet cast me into the seventh circle of hell. Perhaps my name isn't inscribed in the ledger of the damned, after all.

❖ ❖ ❖

The angel of death tries to pour some water into my mouth. No. I mustn't drink this water! "If anyone offers you water when you're in the grave, do not drink of it," Da Mullah Saed Mustafa told my grandfather. On the day of my grandmother's burial, my grandfather recited this commandment so loudly his wife could hear it in her grave:

"Dearly departed! You burn with thirst in the grave. But beware! Satan will come to your grave with a pitcher of water. 'If you want to drink this water, just tell me you have no Creator!' he will whisper in your left ear. And if you keep silent, and if you refuse his water, he will stand on your right and whisper, 'Don't be afraid, I know you are thirsty—here, drink!' But beware, dearly departed! If you drink of Satan's water, you next will speak his words: 'Jesus is the son of God.' Dearly departed, shun Satan! Despise his speech! Cast his water to the ground!"

Satan's water is foul in my mouth. It burns my tongue. I spit it out. The gloom and stench of the grave make my head spin.

I can feel hands stroking my head. They are warm and tender. They are nervous; they tremble.

"Mother, is that you?"

A lock of my mother's hair caresses my face. So soft and gentle.

"Brother, are you awake?"

That's not my mother. Who is it?

Despite all the pain, I force my eyes open. I can't tell whether the blackness I see is her hair or the night. I move my head a fraction. Beneath the dark hair is a woman I do not know. To one side of her, I can make out the face of a child, who says, "Father!"

His hand is stroking my hair.

"Father! You woke up! You came back! Get up!"

Are these the same voices I heard before, the same faces? No, I'm still asleep. I'd better close my eyes again. I close them.

"Stop!"

I stopped. No, I didn't just stop, I froze to the spot. I froze at the sight of a soldier aiming his Kalashnikov right at my head. The soldier was standing in front of a jeep. Its headlights shone straight in my eyes. I put up my hand to stop myself being blinded.

"Stop! Hands behind your head!"

I froze to the spot while the soldier, the gun and the jeep spun around and around in front of my eyes. Then, at the sound of a gun being cocked, everything suddenly lurched to a halt and I turned to stone. Another soldier came around the side of the jeep. His Kalashnikov ready, he walked right up to me and said:

"Password?"

And I said:

"No idea."

"What's the password?" the soldier behind him shouted.

"But what time is it?" I asked, trying to catch a glimpse of my watch.

"Don't move!"

I felt the butt of a Kalashnikov ram into my guts. My mouth filled with blood and I spat out the words:

"The password for the curfew? Sorry, no, I've forgotten."

I tried to lean close to the soldier so I could tell him I'd been drinking, that I was too drunk to remember the password. But the terror of being picked up by the soldiers and then whacked in the stomach by a Kalashnikov was too much for me. Everything went black.

"Down on your knees!"

Those hands that stroked my forehead, that hair brushing against my face, that child who called me "Father," were they really real? Strange how, when you're dreaming, the dream-reality always seems to be more real than reality itself. This is what we are like: our dreams seem more plausible than our lives. But if they didn't, all those revolutions, those wars, those religions and ideologies, could never have been dreamed up . . .

"Brother, can you stand?"

Even though I'm terrified, I open my eyes. Nothing has changed. The same woman, the same child . . .

Morning never comes. Night is an eternity. That woman is here. I am dead. The woman—or angel—is dragging me away. Where is she taking me? To the abyss? How far to the bottom?

My breath stinks of booze, my mouth tastes disgusting. I have sinned. I can feel the wounds to my body that were given to me by Nakir and Munkar as punishment for my sins.

"Dear angel, pardon me! Oh God, have mercy! Save me!"

❖ ❖ ❖

Which one of hell's doors are we going through? Why do the djinn close the door behind us?

"Let go of me, Angel . . ."

The angel lets go of me. I float in midair. I tumble to the ground. I hear nothing but silence.

"Brother, would you like some water?"

I shift my gaze from the face of the new moon to the face of the woman who haunts my nightmare. Here she is, standing above me, a glass of water in her outstretched hand. I lie flat out like a corpse. Wracked with agony. I move my head. I am outside on a terrace. The yellow light of an oil-lamp, shining through the window of a room indoors, illuminates this woman against the backcloth of the night.

No, I am not dreaming. I am not trapped in a nightmare. I am not lost in Barzakh. I am alive and I am awake! Look, I can take the glass from the woman and drink this water . . . I can feel the water coursing through my body. I can feel my burning throat, my aching bones . . . No. This is not a dream. I can clearly make out the slim face of this woman, the dark hair veiling her profile . . .

"Brother, would you like some more water?"

I can understand her too. And I can even reply to her question:

"Thank you!"

Yet the pain prevents me from asking where I am. Or how I got here . . .

The woman disappears down a dark corridor. Then the child emerges from the gloom with a big pillow in his arms.

"Here, Father, put it under your head!"

Why on earth does this child keep calling me "Father"?

The child props the pillow against the wall under the window of the room where the yellow light is shining. I heave myself onto it and collapse. A shadow crosses the terrace. I look behind me. In the lamplight I can make out someone shuffling across the room. He holds his arms away from his sides stiffly, as though they were two withered branches. Then he vanishes into the darkness beyond the door.

Anxiously, I examine the child sitting in front of me who, in turn, is staring at me with a tender smile on his lips. I lie back on the pillow. I close my eyes. I no longer want to think about all these ghosts and dreams.

I succumb to the nightmare.

"Father!"

No, I will never open my eyes again. I believe in my nightmare. I am a prisoner of dreams. I have recited the names of God to no avail.

The nightmare has proved stronger than my faith. My soul is now lost to me.

My grandfather used to say that, according to Da Mullah Saed Mustafa, if your soul ever ventures beyond your control, you should say the name Al-Mumit and then cross your hands on your chest.

I can feel the child's small hand on my forehead.

Al-Mumit. Al-Mumit . . .

"Father, are you better?"

I am tired of all these nightmares. Let me have peace. Peace, are you listening?

The child strokes my forehead. I can see him. He's smiling at me. And suddenly, I want to laugh too—laugh at how helpless I am, laugh at the angels . . . at the djinn . . .

"Yahya, come inside!"

That's Yahya's mother, calling him from down the dark corridor.

"Mother, Father is better; he's smiling."

"I said come inside! It's time for bed!"

The child comes close, and with a look full of tenderness, gives me a kiss on my forehead. Then he scampers off down the corridor in the direction of his mother's voice.

What is going on? What could possibly explain this confusion? Why does this night never come to an end? Who were those soldiers and why did they stop and question me? How did I end up here, with this woman and child? Why does she call me "Brother" and he call me "Father?"

Why haven't they taken me home to my mother?

"Father, drink some juice!"

The child has come back with a glass of juice. With an unsteady hand and a mind brimming with questions, I take the glass from the child and bring it to my lips. The juice stings my mouth, burning my tongue and gums; I feel it swill down my gullet. I can't drink any more; I hand back the glass to the child. I try to move my bruised and battered bones a little, and I ask Yahya to come here. The child, excitedly, sits down next to me. Where do I start?

With asking where I am? Or how I got here? Or why he calls me "Father?"

"Father, where have you been?"

But the child's own question throws me completely. Where on earth have I been?

"Yahya, I said go to bed!"

At the sound of his mother's voice, the child jumps up and runs down the corridor, heading for the light.

Where have I been? Perhaps I've lost my memory! It's not unknown for someone to suffer from amnesia after an accident and to have no idea of who he is or where he comes from. To completely forget his wife, his children, and his home . . . his mind a blank sheet, wiped clean of any familiar names or identifying details . . .

But, no, I do know who I am! My name is Farhad. Mirdad's son. Born in 1337 [1958] . . . My grandfather was a devotee of Da Mullah Saed Mustafa. No one else apart from him was ever allowed to visit Da Mullah Saed Mustafa. Not my grandmother, not my mother. Only my grandfather knew him. Every Friday, after returning from the mosque, my grandfather would call his grandchildren around him, and from under his embroidered cushion he would bring out the Book of the Dead by Imam Ghazali, and then he would begin to read us stories about the afterlife that awaits us when we die. These tales would scare us so much that we'd cry with fear, prostrating ourselves before him, begging to be saved . . .

But these are the very things I was thinking about when I was having that nightmare! And that means, I'm simply repeating my dreams. My mind has gone completely blank and I am taking my nightmare for reality . . .

Ah, but in fact, there are other things I can remember! My mother's name is Humaira. She has three children. My sister Parwaneh and I, and my brother Farid. Two years ago my father took a second wife, younger than my mother. Then, after the coup, he fled to Pakistan. He never divorced my mother, he simply abandoned her . . . Today's date is 24 Mirzan 1358 [October 16, 1979]. Not long ago, Hafizullah Amin, that faithful student of Taraki, murdered his own dear teacher and put himself in power . . . What else?

No, my memory is intact! I've never been married, nor had any children. So far—other than in my intense fantasies when I masturbate—I've yet to experience the delight of a woman's tender embrace . . .

So, I've got no reason to think I've lost my memory! Nor to question my identity or doubt my history. No. Something has happened. Probably a mistake. Well, we'll see. Maybe I drank too much again—so much that it's poisoned my mind and made everything seem like a very vivid nightmare.

"Brother, you must be hungry. Would you like something to eat?"

The woman stands in the doorway holding an oil-lamp. The lamplight throws the pleats of her skirt into sharp relief, but her face is concealed by the darkness of the corridor.

Yes, I am hungry. But I can't face eating any food. I'm hungry to know where I am and how I got here.

"No, thank you, Sister . . . but . . ."

Suddenly, the ghost whose shadow I saw a few minutes ago, walking across the room, emerges from the darkness behind her, moaning. At the sight of his two bowed arms, like withered branches attached to his body, my question dies in my mouth. The woman, unmoved by his arrival, takes the strange phantom's hand and leads him back down the corridor.

Once again I'm left alone with a hundred-and-one unanswered questions, helpless in the house of a stranger.

My best friend, Enayat, and I decided to pay a visit to Moalem's shop. There, as always, we found the old man with his misshapen figure and his long, flowing hair wedged behind a counter laden with potatoes and chick-peas. And, as always, he winked at us, shooing off the two children who were haggling over a sack of beans. Then his smile broadened into a grin, his eyes twinkled with mischief and he announced in a quavering voice that echoed all around his humble little shop, "The Daughters of the Vine await your command!"

Tottering gingerly to the back of the shop on his unsteady legs, he tugged back a black-and-white curtain and invited us into his den.

"Always drink in secret, for those they find they punish cruelly!"

He laughed loudly, closing the curtain behind us to hide us from sight, then plumped himself down in front of two clay pitchers.

"Do you fancy the blonde or the redhead?" he asked, turning to me.

"The redhead."

"Well chosen!"

He poured red wine from the pitcher into a cheap metal cup and, taking the first mouthful himself, shook his old head and said, "Oh, if only Hafez were here, he'd dedicate a poem to me! Drink deeply and see what miracles can be found in the world."

He refilled the cup with red wine and handed it to me. Then he turned to Enayat.

"Redhead or blonde?"

"The blonde."

"Another excellent choice."

He poured out white wine from the other pitcher, drank it himself, as before, and shaking his head again said, "Oh, if only I'd lived in the time of Babur, he would have planted half of Kabul with vines just for me!"

Then he refilled the cup with white wine and handed it to Enayat. We drank until nightfall, then we took Moalem home, holding him up between us. His sleepy wife opened the door and swore at her husband, and us. She told us to dump him on the terrace, grumbling, "I can never tell whether you go around there to buy drink from him or just to get him drunk."

Moalem's laughter floated over his small backyard.

"*There was a man . . . a rotten drunk . . . who traded wine . . .*"

"Like Shams," his wife shouted back at him, "God will never let you rest on this earth!"

But Moalem continued his slurred performance:

"Someone asked . . . That's strange . . . If you're selling wine . . . what could you want in return?"

Moalem's wife threw us out of the house and we fetched up near Enayat's place, in the middle of the garden belonging to the Party headquarters. It was pitch dark. Enayat decided we should piss on the roots of this big cherry tree, so our piss would find its way into the red cherries. So we pissed at the tree, and pissed ourselves laughing.

But the night watchman spoiled our fun and, waving his gun at us, chucked us out of the garden. I parted with Enayat by the gate and he vanished off into the night. The curfew went clean out of my head. Halfway home, a soldier's command froze me to the spot.

"Stop!"

I'm running. I'm running through the night. Quick as a breeze. Carbonized trees bearing desiccated cherries line both sides of the road, leading me on. The road is endless. I run. A soldier runs after me, pounding the ground with his big heavy boots, bellowing, "STOP! STOP!"

But I do not stop. I run. Faster than an arrow. I grow bigger with each stride. Bigger and bigger. I'm taller than the trees. The soldier dwindles away. He gets smaller and smaller. I stop to piss on the soldier. But, as I piss, the soldier starts getting bigger. Bigger and bigger! I can't piss anymore. The soldier is laughing at me. I am crying. My sniveling sounds as though it's coming from somewhere small inside my chest. The soldier's laughter booms through the night. He claps his big hand on my shoulder. My shoulder feels paralyzed. He shakes me like a doll.

"Brother!"

The night is even darker than when my eyes are closed. I move my head in the direction of the sound. Then, out of the dark, suddenly lamplight illuminates strands of hair that have fallen in front of my face. I pull back my head. And, once again, I see the same woman whose child calls me "Father." I look around. I'm where I was before. On a small terrace under a window.

The woman tucks her hair behind her ear. The lamplight reveals her face.

"Brother, get up! Quick!"

"What . . ."

What should I say? The woman wants to tell me something.

"Quick, get inside! The soldiers have come back!"

A sudden cacophony of slammed jeep doors, barked military orders, and jackboots hitting the cobblestones ricochets round the street below. The mother of the child whose name I still don't know extinguishes the lamp. Crouching down beside me, she goes completely still. In the dark, in agony, I try to heave myself onto my feet.

She rises up next to me and, gingerly, silently, glides toward the entrance to the house, beckoning me with the two fingers that had scooped back the hair from her eyes. I stagger to my feet and drag my broken body along after her, into the absolute darkness of the corridor. She closes the door behind us and is lost in the dark.

"Come in here!"

Blindly, I follow the rustle of her skirts. The sound moves into a room. And stops. A struck match flares up, canceling the dark. She lights an old candle whose wax has spilt an extravagant fringe all over the windowsill. It is a small room with a black-and-red carpet and two big floor cushions, one by the door, the other under the

44

window. I kick off my shit-caked shoes and lower myself onto the cushion by the door as the woman goes back to the corridor.

"Stay here a minute."

"Sorry to . . ."

Why did I say that? The woman has vanished.

I feel as feeble as the faltering candle.

Night has finished the candle. In the pitch-black room, my anxiety grows so extreme that, eventually, shaking with fear, I force myself to raise the curtain a tiny bit to see if the soldiers are down in the courtyard. But it's dark, silent, utterly deserted. Where has the woman gone? What made the soldiers come here? Are they looking for me? But what am I supposed to have done?

I must get out of here. My mother hasn't the faintest clue what's happened to me. Right this very minute she's sitting behind our front door in the hope of hearing my footsteps coming up the street. But she doesn't hear me. Now and then she peers around the door, straining this way and that, desperate to see me emerge from the gloom. But she doesn't see me. She wrings her hands. She recites verses from the Koran under her breath. She frowns. She bites her lip. She solemnly promises to make offerings at the Shah-Do-Shamshira Mosque if I turn up safe and sound. I must go.

I feel my way to the door. I know where my discarded shoes are from their terrible stench and, holding them in one hand, I creep on tiptoe into the corridor.

"Where are you going?"

I drop the shoes in shock. The woman is standing behind the glass door of the corridor.

"I must get out of here!"

"Where are you going?"

"Home."

"Now? The street is full of soldiers!"

The woman walks past me toward a half-opened door from which pale yellow lamplight spills out into the gloom of the corridor. Before going through it, she looks back for an instant through her disheveled hair; then she speaks to me softly, in a way that suddenly makes me long to hear my mother's voice:

"Put your shoes on."

In the time that it takes me to put on my shoes, she goes into the room and returns with the oil-lamp in one hand. With the other, she leads the phantom I saw earlier, his arms still strangely arched from his sides. Now I can see his face. His hair and his beard are pure white. But he's not old. He's very young. Maybe even younger than I am.

"Come on, follow me."

At the sound of her voice I stop staring at his prematurely whitened hair, and instead try to make out the far end of the corridor from where I can hear her skirts rustle. She opens a little door that leads to the back of the house. We climb down a narrow flight of stairs. At the bottom of the staircase she sweeps straw and earth with her bare

47

hands from a secret trapdoor. Easing it open, she asks me to go down first.

I descend without a moment's hesitation, without even asking myself—or her—what I'm doing.

I enter a rectangular-shaped hole, closely followed by the ghost, who squeezes in next to me. The woman closes the door above us and we hear the scratching sound of straw being scattered over our heads. Or maybe no one else hears this but me.

Who is this ghost? Her husband? Or just an unknown passerby like me, whom she has sheltered and cared for? Maybe I'll stay here too, like him and, like his, my hair will also turn white. What can she want from us?

They're banging on the front door. The ghost's breath comes faster, heavier. The smell of the shit on my shoes cuts through the dank, underground aroma of the hole. The sound of jackboots echoes faintly from the courtyard. The ghost whimpers quietly to himself, very quietly. Beads of cold sweat break out on my forehead and slide down my nose, one by one. I feel liquid lap around my feet. The ghost whines more urgently. A current of warm, moist air rises from the ground, then the sharp tang of urine. The ghost has pissed himself. His moans get louder.

Quite a cocktail: piss and shit; soft moans and sharp breaths; pain and pitch dark.

Buried alive, here in my grave.

My grandfather used to say that, according to Da Mullah Saed Mustafa, the evil deeds of sinners and infidels turn into blind and starving wolves that come to visit them in the grave. The wolves then ravage them until the day of judgment.

Or they turn into filthy, rancid pigs that rut and torture them . . .

Yes, I am a sinner. And to torture me now that I'm dead, they've sent down an angel who is blind and deaf so he can neither respond to my cries of agony nor witness the pain etched on my face.

Where is the winding-sheet inscribed with my sins?

"Brother?"

If I ever open my eyes again—I open them—there'll be nothing to see but the usual darkness . . . and here it is. Alongside the identical stink of shit and piss and sick, the changeless reek of the grave . . . the familiar moans of the white-haired ancient-young man . . . the blind ghost, the deaf ghost . . . and the woman who tells me, "Brother, come on, you can come out of there!"

Again I must move. But I can't. Again the woman must sprinkle my face with water; my eyes must open; I must raise myself out of the grave of this tight box-shaped earth burrow; I must climb stairs, tread the dark and endless passage, return to the tiny room that isn't mine, collapse onto the floor . . . and I must hear the woman tell me:

"Brother, the soldiers have gone . . ."

And then I must close my eyes, again.

I come around to the sound of pitiful whining. I open my eyes. Nothing to be seen. I put my hand on the floor: no shit, no dirt. The thick pile of a carpet. The moans are more urgent. A door shudders open; yellow light floods into the corridor; a shaft falls into this room. The light moves. Another door scrapes open and the light is gone. The plaintive cries come to a stop. A soft glow bathes the corridor.

I'm very thirsty. My throat is on fire, my head is pounding. The putrid smells of shit and piss and sick and blood and wine still cling to me. I need to drink some water. I get up. The gentle light from a half-open door leads me on, light that has abandoned this room full of pain and instead has banished night from the heart of the corridor. I reach the door. The oil-lamp rests on the threshold. At the other end of the room the mother of the child who called me "Father" is sitting on the floor. She has taken her breast out of her blouse. Her nipple is in the mouth of the white-haired ghost, who is sucking like a baby.

I close my eyes. I take a breath. I open them. No, I'm not dreaming. The ghost is sucking on the woman's white breast. I want to move. I can't. My feet are fixed to the floor. The ghost closes his eyes. The woman tenderly lifts his white head from her breast and rests it on a cushion.

She mustn't see me. I have to go. But I'm transfixed. She tucks her exposed breast back inside her blouse. I'm frozen to the spot. She gets up and walks toward the door. I break out in a cold sweat. Picking up the lamp, she steps out into the corridor. The ordeal of the night sinks onto my shoulders. She stands in front of me. I am paralyzed. She says nothing.

"Where's the bathroom?" I ask.

The woman tucks her hair behind her ear. There's not a hint of nervousness, surprise, or shame about her. Holding the oil-lamp aloft, she leads me to a small open door, goes in to put down the lamp then comes back into the corridor.

"I'll go and find you some clean clothes and a towel."

The mirror scares the life out of me. In its reflection I see a ghost whose hair has not yet gone white. Is that really me?

I toss my filthy clothes, covered in blood and vomit, into a corner, take the lamp, leave the bathroom, and go back to the room.

The woman is sitting on the cushion by the door. Neither the sudden light of the oil-lamp nor my return stops her from staring at the carpet. Her head hanging down, her hair, as always, curtaining half her face. She is silent. I leave the lamp close to the door, within her reach, and moving very carefully so as not to disturb her, I go over to the cushion under the windowsill. From the corpse of the old candle, a new light burns. I sit down. My shadow trembles on the opposite wall, over the woman's body.

I gaze, transfixed, at the black lines on the carpet, haunted by the desire to cast a quick glance at her. Is her breast still uncovered?

We sit in silence. Each of us waiting for the other to speak. Should I say something? But what? Who are you? Why have you mixed me up with somebody else? Why won't you let me go? All these questions, right on the tip of my tongue, make my heart pound, my stomach churn, my throat seize up.

❖ ❖ ❖

I'm spellbound by the patterns on the carpet. I must say something.

"Sister, I can't begin to thank you for everything you've done for me. But the truth is, I have no idea what on earth has happened to me! Yesterday . . ."

"My son, Yahya, and I were sitting outside on the terrace when we heard a jeep pull up, and then soldiers cursing and shouting—followed by the sound of someone being kicked and punched. After they'd gone, I went into the street and found you passed out in the sewer."

My mesmerized gaze, now freed from the patterns on the carpet, falls instead on the flowers printed on the cushion beneath her. But it lacks the courage to travel any further up her body . . .

"Yes . . . I was out late. After curfew. I was on my way home . . . I've caused you so much trouble . . . I really should be going now."

The woman's hand is hiding a flower on the cushion.

"You should stay here till morning; we can sort things out tomorrow. You're safe here—they've already searched the place thoroughly so they won't be coming back. I have a suspicion it was you they were after. They said a burglar had gone to ground around here. They've turned the whole area upside down."

My gaze, stricken with guilt, moves hesitantly upward, away from the woman's hand covering the flower pattern.

"They were looking for a burglar?"

Her blouse is done up.

"Well, they had to come up with something to convince us to go along with the search."

One half of her face is hidden by my shadow, the other by her hair.

"I have no idea why they arrested me and beat me up. All I did was forget the password!"

Releasing the crumpled flower on the cushion, her hand lifts her hair from one side of her face, and tucks it behind her ear. And I shift my head away from the candle, lifting my shadow from the other side of her face.

"Not having the password or the Party membership card is a crime in itself."

"Oh no! My ID card and student card!"

Without thinking, I leap up and rush to the bathroom where I hurriedly search through my trousers and shirt pockets. Nothing. Dejected and exhausted, I return to the room. The woman is sitting on the cushion as calm as ever. Frantic with worry, I stay standing by the door.

"I have to go."

"Without your ID?"

"They've probably chucked my documents in the sewer; they wouldn't have hung on to them."

"Are you suggesting you go and look for them now? They're patrolling the streets."

Confused, I take a few steps back to the cushion under the window. In complete disarray, I cry out under my breath:

"Mother!"

"I'll fetch you something to eat," the woman says as if she hasn't noticed a thing.

She rises to her feet. Picking up the oil-lamp, she unsettles the silence of the dark passageway.

Like the melting wax of the candle on the windowsill, I sink down onto the cushion once more.

Alone again, I'm haunted by the image of my mother's face, her worry hidden from my brother and sister because it's still night. They must sleep. They've got to go to school in the morning. My mother paces back and forth behind the door to the street, praying all the while. The courtyard is taut with her anxiety. I must go, otherwise my mother will stay up all night.

"I have to go!"

My voice rends the cavernous silence of the room. I get up. My shadow shatters all over the walls and ceiling. Yahya's mother comes in from the corridor, carrying a tray.

"I have to go!"

"Have something to eat first."

The woman kneels down to pour the tea. Her manner as unruffled as ever, just like her untroubled gaze, her steady speech.

"My mother won't be able to sleep."

"If you leave now and fall into the hands of the soldiers, your dear mother will never sleep again."

I am at her mercy. I feel like a child. Shaking as violently as my shadow, I sit down on the floor by the tray. The woman busies herself with the tea.

"Sister, I've caused you more than enough trouble already. You . . ."

The woman drops a sugar cube into a glass of tea and hands me some bread.

"Let me assure you, it's impossible to imagine anything worse than what I've been through these past few years. There's nothing darker than total darkness."

Her even gaze travels slowly across my trembling shadow.

"A year ago, my husband was thrown into jail. Then came the news that he'd been executed. I haven't told Yahya. He thinks his father has gone on a journey to a faraway city called Pul-e-Charkhi . . ."

"Why does he call me 'Father'? Do I look like his father?"

"No, you're nothing like him."

"Then why?" I want to ask. Has he forgotten what his father looks like? Aren't there any photos of his father in the house? What was going on when he announced, triumphantly, that he'd woken me out of my dreams?

Yahya's mother slumps back against the wall and disappears into her shadow. Her eyes track the movement of my hand. I put the bread down on the tray. Her gaze locks on the bread.

"The young man who was with you in that hole is my brother. He's not yet eighteen. He was in prison for three weeks. I don't know what on earth they did to him there.

His mind is gone. His hair turned white overnight. Now, he never says a word. Every night he wakes up, moaning and sobbing like a newborn child . . ."

She falls silent, her eyes fixed on my trembling hand as it replaces the glass of tea on the tray. In my mind's eye I see her naked breast, as innocent as my mother's, fill with tears.

"Two times they've called him up to the army. They're convinced he's faking. Each time he's come back more damaged than before. All I can do now is try to hide him away."

She tucks her hair behind one ear. Silence. As though she is waiting for me to start asking all those unasked questions. But I too am silent.

Then, abruptly, she gets up, loading all my questions, my fears, and my feelings onto the tray with the bread and the tea, and she carries them off into the darkness of the corridor.

Yahya's mother comes back to say "Sleep well," then leaves me with my quaking shadow. I focus on the image of her fingertips gathering up her hair. Fingertips that, when I'm most afraid, seem to sweep my fear away with that lock of hair she tucks behind one ear.

What is it about this simple gesture that leaves me mesmerized and tongue-tied—and banishes all my doubts?

It moves me because, through this effortless movement, she reveals herself to me. When her face is hidden by her hair, I worry that she's anxious. But when she lifts it back, I can see she's not afraid.

"You should beware of two things about a woman: her hair and her tears."

God knows why my grandfather told my father that.

He muttered prayers to himself as he fingered three of his worry beads, then continued:

"Her hair will chain you and her tears will drown you!"

Another three beads, another three prayers, and then:

"That's why it's imperative they cover up their hair and their faces!"

He said this on the day my father decided to take a second wife. My mother wept—and then her face once again assumed its mask of fear.

My grandmother used to say that my mother was born with a terrified face, and it was the face I was used to. Whenever someone met her for the first time, they'd assume she was scared of them.

I couldn't understand what it was exactly that made her appear so frightened. Was it because her face looked so drawn and thin? Or because of the dark circles under her eyes? Or because her mouth turned down at the corners? If my mother ever smiled, she would smile between the two deep lines cut into her face like the brackets around a sentence; if she ever cried, she would cry between brackets. In fact she lived her whole life between brackets . . .

But, one day, the brackets vanished. The terrified mask dropped from her face. And then, a few months later, my father took a second wife. No one asked why, because even if someone had dared to ask, my father would never have answered.

My father had no interest whatsoever in why my mother always looked so frightened. He couldn't have, otherwise how could he have lived alongside a woman who always looked so terrified? Truth is, my father never loved my mother at all, he just fucked her. He'd get on top of her in the dark, close his eyes . . . and get on with it.

But what happened the day the fear vanished from my mother's face to make my father think about taking another wife? Probably my father needed a woman to be scared of him in order to get turned on. And the day my mother stopped being terrified of having sex, my father's desire vanished. So he had to get himself another wife. A younger wife who'd still be scared of sex.

And maybe the day my mother lost her fear of having sex was the first time she ever enjoyed it. The first and last time.

But it wasn't long before she put her frightened mask back on. This time not because she was scared of having sex, but because she was terrified he'd leave her.

Tonight, lonelier than ever, my brave mother has placed her frightened face behind the street door while she waits for me to come home.

Her worn-out hands, free at night to be raised to beg God's mercy, recite the prayer for safe return.

I must go.

"Where are you going?"

The woman's voice hits me just as I reach the far side of the terrace. I can't look at her face. I stare pathetically at the door in front of me, and weakly offer:

"I have to go home."

Under her gaze, once again, I feel like a child—small and pitiful.

"You want to go—go then! But take great care the soldiers never find out that I took you in."

I abandon my mother behind our door. I let her recite her prayers as many times as the stars she counts in the sky with her mouth enclosed in its brackets.

Like a naughty boy, my eyes fixed on the ground, I turn back to the terrace. I don't dare look at the fingers that gather the hair from the side of the woman's face to tuck it behind her ear.

I freeze at the door to the corridor.

"Sister . . ."

"Mahnaz. My name is Mahnaz. I hate being called 'Sister.' And you—what's your name?"

"Farhad . . . I just wanted to say that I have no desire to put your life in danger . . ."

"At the moment it's far more dangerous for me if you leave than if you stay. We will find a way tomorrow."

I walk back down the corridor. I take my shoes off. I enter the room I just left.

Night deals with the candle.

If mine doesn't stand up
If yours doesn't stand up
If his doesn't stand up
Then who will fuck the mothers of our nation?

Enayat condemned himself to exile with this variation on
a favorite theme of the Communist Party. He'd written
his little ditty on a scrap of paper that he folded in four
and then tossed to me in class. Of course, it landed at the
feet of a Communist-Party student who, of course, read
it—and immediately recognized Enayat's handwriting.

Before the lecture had finished, Enayat was gone from the
campus.

That night I went around to his house. My best friend
had decided to flee the country.

We spent the next two nights together, saying farewell
to Kabul. It was to be a very poetic farewell. We got drunk
on both nights. We slept not a wink.

Enayat had wanted me to be at his side for his last Kabul
sunrise. At the moment when night finally dies under the

boots of the night-watchman, and dreams are interrupted by the mullah's call to prayer, Enayat and I were lost in the vineyards of Bagh-e-Bala. Waiting for sunup had made us thirsty, so Enayat drank dew from the leaves of each vine. Enayat was no poet, but he knew how to behave in true poetic fashion.

After the sun rose, we went back home and drank yet more wine. When our wine ran out, we returned to Moalem's shop, in search of the Daughters of the Vine.

The night has consumed all but the stub of the candle. Mechanically I move my hand toward the flame. If it burns me, I'll know I'm awake.

None of this really makes any sense. Maybe because I don't want it to make any sense. Maybe because I'd rather I were having a nightmare than living my life.

My little finger hurts.

I wish that Mahnaz—for all her extraordinary kindness and generosity—were merely a dream. I wish that when I opened my eyes, I'd find myself in my room at home, watching dawn break on my mother's lined face as she whispers a prayer above my head, while she wafts the fresh morning air over me . . . I wish she were holding me tight . . .

She holds us both in her arms, Farid and me. We're both very small. Farid cries out:

"Father! Father!"

Who's he calling "Father"? Me?

"No Farid, it's me! I'm your brother!"

Farid won't listen. He continues sobbing. My mother takes out her breasts and pushes a nipple into each of our mouths. Without saying a word. Farid begins to suck at my mother's breast, but then he pulls back. His mouth is filled with blood. I stare at my mother's breast. Instead of milk, blood spurts out. But I still suck her other breast. There is no smell of blood. Only the smell of milk. But it's milk that's gone off! I turn away from my mother's breast. Sour milk surges up my throat into my mouth.

"Mother, Father is being sick again!" Farid shouts.

The smell of vomit overwhelms me. Then I see Yahya standing in front of me. He jumps up and heads down the corridor calling to his mother.

"Mother, Father is throwing up!"

Mahnaz appears at the door with a cloth in her hand. She sits down next to me and puts the damp cloth on my forehead. After a huge effort—using all the power I no longer possess—I manage to move myself. Mahnaz helps me sit up. The shirt that must have belonged either to Mahnaz's mute, damaged brother or to her murdered husband is covered with vomit. She dabs my mouth and face clean. I avoid her eyes. I have the impression her breasts are uncovered. I fix my gaze on her hands, hands that with such tenderness gently wipe my face and neck.

"Do you feel a little better now?"

"Yes . . ."

Both of them are so sweet and kind! What do they want from me?

Yahya hands me a glass of water and sits down before me.

"Are you all right, Father?"

"Yahya, leave Farhad alone! Go into the other room!"

Mahnaz cleans up my vomit from the carpet. I should help her. But I can't. The child gets up and leaves the room. I want to say something. But my tongue is heavy. I am still staring at Mahnaz's hands. My heart beats more fiercely than ever. It pounds with utter exhaustion, it thumps with things unsaid . . . Mahnaz stands up.

"The curfew is over. I'll go and get you some medicine."

"Please don't go to any trouble . . . Really, I'll be fine . . ."

Mahnaz leaves the room.

Morning waits outside the window. It waits for the curtains to be drawn so it can slip into this room where I am waiting.

I will not draw back those curtains.

Daylight streams through the gap between the curtains, spilling onto the windowsill and down over the cushion that I'm sitting on, illuminating the black patterns woven into the deep red pile of the carpet. Mahnaz has gone out to get some bread for breakfast, and some medicine for me. Yahya sits on the cushion by the door. We both are silent. The child's trusting face mocks me. He doesn't look anything like me! Actually, he looks nothing like his mother, either. Which means he must take after his father. But, if that's the case, why would he mistake me for him?

I trawl the blank white walls of the room searching for a photograph of his father. On the windowsill, next to the candle stub, are two large books with gold inlaid covers. I take down both of them. One is *Haft Paikar* and the other *Khosraw & Sheerin*. I put them back on the windowsill.

Why does Yahya call me "Father"? Mahnaz never answered my question. Maybe he's never seen his father.

I call him over to me. He springs up with excitement and sits down in front of me, right in the middle of the sunbeam that falls onto the carpet through the gap between the curtains. He looks at me intently, unquestioningly. Yet the mind of a child like Yahya should be full of questions, particularly for someone he calls "Father!" A father who's been missing for ages and has suddenly come back beaten to a pulp! Last night he asked me only one question—"Father, where have you been?"—and he did not wait for my answer. He left. It was a question without a question mark. He didn't even repeat it. But I'll be gone in a short while. He needs to understand that I'm not his father, that I'll be going away, that . . .

"Yahya, I . . ."

The child moves his right eye out of the sunbeam. A constant smile on his face. Nothing in the way he looks at me gives me any impression that he's eager for me to continue. On the contrary, he looks at me as though there's an entirely different conversation going on inside his head: "For heaven's sake, please leave me to my imagination. I know you're not my father. But can't we pretend for a while? Just as you want to imagine that everything that's happened here is nothing other than a terrible nightmare, I need to inhabit the dream that my father has returned. Please don't spoil it!"

"Father, I know where you've been!"

He says this like he's revealing an incredible secret, in a voice that matches the secretive look on his face.

"You do? Where have I been?"

He wriggles his little body closer to mine.

"You've been in the city of Pul-e-Charkhi."

"And what's it like there?"

He fingers the sunbeam, then traces the flower-pattern on the cushion.

"It's a very big city with a huge bridge in the middle—and the bridge spins around and around all the time."

"Can you remember when I went away?"

"No, because I was fast asleep. The lamps had run out of oil. My mother said you'd gone out to get us some oil. Then you got lost and nobody recognized you there. You left your ID card at home so you got stuck and you couldn't come back. The bridge wouldn't stop spinning. When I asked Uncle Anwar when you'd be able to get off the bridge and leave Pul-e-Charkhi, he said: 'In a dream!'"

The child stops playing with the sunbeam and the flowers on the cushion.

"My mother cried. She thought you would never come back again. But just like Uncle Anwar said, at night you came back in my dreams, although you'd disappear before we woke up. So I promised my mother that one night when you came into my dream I'd catch you and I wouldn't let you go away again!"

The child has caught me in his dream. I am a dream-creature. I am an imaginary father, an imaginary husband . . . So why bother going back to my life?

❖ ❖ ❖

I leave Yahya in his silent dreams of a city with a huge bridge that spins around and around for ever, and I close my eyes only to find myself in someone else's dream—in the feverish dreams of my mother.

My mother hasn't slept a wink. She's even forgotten her morning prayers. Now that the curfew is over, she ventures outdoors to wait at the end of the street. But I'm nowhere to be seen. She goes back indoors. Where else can she go? Who would know where I might have gone? She goes to Enayat's house. But I'm not there. Then what? Which department should she go to first—should she go to the Ministry?

"Over there, Mother, wait in the queue!"

She walks past another hundred mothers to find a place at the end of the queue. She smiles at the soldier for me. She calls him "Brother."

"Dear Brother, Farhad son of Mirdad did not come home last night . . ."

"Well, he's not here. He's gone, he's fled with the rest of them . . ."

"Gone. Fled." She repeats the words over and over between her bracketed lips. "Gone where? Fled where? Why didn't he say anything?"

How could I possibly leave my mother, Farid, and Parwaneh behind?

My mother has never forgotten how, when my father walked out on her and left her with three children, I cursed him—his cowardice and cruelty—to heaven and earth.

"No, he can't have left us! But where on earth can he have gone? Has the army got hold of him? Is he in prison?"

She swallows her fear, covering her mouth with both hands to stop herself crying out loud. She decides to wait it out in a corner, under the sympathetic gaze of all the other mothers . . .

I have to go! I get up. Yahya watches me with his penetrating gaze. I take a few steps toward the corridor.

"Father, Mother's coming back soon."

Right. I must leave before Mahnaz gets back. I don't want the look on her face to deflect my intentions. Where are my shoes? I look in the corridor. They're nowhere to be seen. Have they hidden them away? I go back to the room. Yahya still sits there in silence, smiling to himself at my feeble attempt to escape.

"Where are my shoes?"

The child gets up calmly. With a tremulous look, full of longing for me to stay put, he walks past me down the corridor onto the terrace. He returns carrying my shoes.

"My mother cleaned them for you."

He puts my shoes down next to my feet and goes back to the room to sit on the cushion by the door and stare at my hesitant feet. The shoes are still damp. Never mind. My mother is waiting.

I hate having to walk out on Yahya. His plaintive stare is paralyzing. I move purposefully across the courtyard toward the door to the street. The door opens. It is Mahnaz.

"Where are you going?"

She hurriedly shuts the door behind her. The smell of fresh bread fills the courtyard.

"I have to go."

"Off you go then—go!"

She opens the door a little, just enough for me to see two soldiers lounging in the street. The sight of their jackboots makes my desire to leave vanish instantly. I jerk back. Mahnaz shuts the door. We walk back across the courtyard.

"I was under the impression that I've been sheltering an ordinary young man who's simply dodging the draft. But tell me, who are you?"

"Trust me, Mahnaz, I'm no one at all."

"So why are they still looking for you?"

"I have no idea! I keep asking myself that, too. All night I've been thinking about everything I've done in the past couple of days—and nothing can explain it. I'm no rebel; I've got no connection to the resistance, to jihad, or to revolution . . . I was hanging out with a friend who was having to get out of Kabul. After we parted I was simply walking back home. Sure, it was late, well after curfew, and the night patrol caught me. But it was nothing, nothing serious . . . The only thing I can think of is that I made the mistake of calling an ordinary officer 'Commander'—and that he thought maybe I was making a fool of him . . ."

I walk close to Mahnaz. I want to look at her discreetly.

Whether or not she believes my story is hidden under her hair. I keep quiet.

We reach the corridor. Mahnaz and Yahya go to the kitchen. I return to the room I was in. I take off my damp shoes and sit down once more on the cushion under the windowsill.

What am I frightened of? Why do I always give in to this woman? Is her disapproval more important than my mother's anxiety? No! Then what? What's stopping me from leaving? I'm out of here.

I get up from the cushion. My heart is pounding.

I am nobody. All I have to do is go to the Party's district office and give them an explanation of what happened last night. I'll tell them it's all a mistake. I had no intention whatsoever of insulting an officer. I'd had a bit too much to drink and I was out of control. If I've caused any offense, I'm ready to offer a full apology.

I put my damp shoes on again in the corridor. My heart thumps more than ever.

She steps out of the kitchen into the corridor carrying a plate on a tray that gives off the aroma of breakfast.

"Why don't you sit down in there?"

With one look into her eyes I am powerless. The decision to leave deflates into my sodden shoes. Why can't I just tell her I want to go? Why doesn't she understand that if anyone finds me here I am done for! And what about you? You're a widowed woman. Your husband was a political prisoner! Are we related? No. So what kind of relationship could I possibly be having with a woman who's not only a complete stranger but who's also a widow? If your family finds out I've been here, then how on earth will you explain why you've given shelter to a young man you know nothing about?

Mahnaz leaves me with a head full of questions and a paralyzed tongue. She has placed the tray beside the cushion under the window and has gone back to the corridor where she disappears into her brother's room. I return to this room and sit on the cushion. On the tray next to the cup of tea, Mahnaz has left some pills to calm nausea.

Yes, I do feel nauseous.

But not because of what I have eaten. I am sick with fear.

I'd gone to the university library to take out the *Book of Shams*, but the librarian told me someone else was reading it. So I borrowed another book and, having given it a quick glance, sat down. At the far end of the table was a young man wearing a pair of dark glasses. His head was buried in a book and he looked as though he wanted to devour every word. Since it happened to be the one I was after, I sidled up to him and coughed, so politely that even I could barely hear myself.

"Excuse me, but would you mind letting me know when you've finished with that book . . ." I whispered.

Lifting his intense gaze from the page he was scrutinizing, he shot me a look, loaded with the passion of the words he was consuming. He gave me a quick nod and once more buried his small head in the big book.

After a while he looked up again and wrote something in the margins of his book. Then he indicated to me with a gesture that he'd finished reading. We went up to the desk together so I could take the book out, and then I returned to the table. The first thing I did was look for the page that he'd written on. He'd underlined the words,

"We cannot speak. But if only we could hear! Speech has no meaning without a listener. But ears are sealed, hearts are stopped, tongues are fettered . . . " And at the margin of the page, in pencil, he had written: "= annihilation."

The same day, in the university café, I found the scribe of the *Book of Shams*. We chatted together over a cup of tea. His name was Enayat.

What else can you call those moments of nameless terror other than "annihilation?" Those moments when you begin to doubt your very existence. When you're so paralyzed with fear that you turn to fantasies for reassurance, to imaginary women, to djinn, to angels, to life after death . . .

I'd managed to empty my head of those phantoms a very long time ago. The djinn were nothing more than children's games in a play directed by my grandfather, and the afterlife was a cover-story dreamt up by the human terror of nonexistence . . .

But the butts of those Kalashnikovs summoned up my slumbering grandfather and the long-forgotten djinn and set them center-stage once more. I'd much rather believe in the reality of their performance than in the utter abeyance of annihilation!

Yes, I do believe in the journey of my soul, in the existence of the djinn, in the finality of death—but I cannot believe what I'm going through right now . . .

"Farhad, have you got a phone at home?"

With the aid of a swig of tea, I manage to swallow the dry bread in my mouth, and without looking at Mahnaz's face framed by the doorway, I answer, "No! But . . ."

"Then give me your address!"

I get up and move toward the door.

"Please, my dear Mahnaz, really, you've done more than enough . . ."

"I want to know your address."

Reluctantly, I tell her.

"I won't be long."

She leaves. I remain fixed to the spot. Before opening the door out of the corridor, Mahnaz pauses to call Yahya. He comes running from his mother's bedroom.

"Yahya, don't open the door to anyone!"

She leaves the corridor. Takes a few steps on the terrace. And returns to the house. I move closer to the doorway.

"Is there anything you want me to tell your mother?"

"No . . . but . . ."

I cannot go on. I want to insist that I will go myself, that . . .

"You'll have to go before midday. Please don't leave the house until I get back. I don't want anyone to know you're here."

She turns to go on her way. I stand by the window. Mahnaz opens the street door and disappears. Yahya waits for me in the doorway to the room.

Perhaps I have landed in a city that spins forever around a giant bridge.

Mahnaz should have reached our street by now. She must have asked directions at the bakery:

"Can you tell me where Farhad's house is? His mother is a teacher, Humaira."

Safdar, known as "Long Fingers," has pulled his head out of the clay oven, wiped the sweat from his brow, and said, "First street on the left, second house, the wooden door with no paint."

At the mention of my name, as always, Safdar's brother stops kneading the dough, and his sweet voice calls from the far end of the bakery, *"Last night the sound of Farhad's chisel never reached us from Mount Beysitoun . . . It's into the dreams of Sheerin that Farhad now has gone . . ."*

Mahnaz is standing outside our door. Without a moment's delay she presses the bell, but she can't hear it ring. She's forgotten that there's been no electricity in Kabul for some time now. After a minute, she rattles the chain on the door. And then she hears the voice of Parwaneh or Farid ask from behind the door, "Who is it?"

What should she say?

"I've got news from Farhad."

There's a brief silence and then Parwaneh or Farid opens the door halfway, and gives Mahnaz a curious look.

My mother's exhausted, hopeless voice calls from the courtyard, "Who is it?"

Parwaneh—or Farid—pushes the door nearly shut. No, why would they close the door? Their eyes fixed on Mahnaz, brimming with curiosity, they call back to my mother, "It's someone with news of Farhad."

My mother runs to the door. If she trips on the loose tile, for the first time ever she will forget to curse me for not having mended it. Her frightened face appears at the door. She doesn't open it completely. Peering around the half-opened door, she examines Mahnaz from top to toe. She doesn't dare ask, "What has happened to him?"

"My name is Mahnaz. I've come on behalf of Farhad."

Who on earth is Mahnaz? Why have I never said anything about this girl? She sizes up Mahnaz. She is not short. So she's not a liar. She has a steady gaze. My mother opens the door to Mahnaz. She asks her in. Before shutting the door, she scans the street in both directions with an anxious look. She closes the door. She fixes her dark-ringed, sleepless eyes on those of Mahnaz. Mahnaz understands my mother's terrified, questioning look and immediately reassures her. She says that I'm fine, safe and sound, but I've had to hide in her house. What am I doing hiding in this woman's house? Is there anything going on between us? Mahnaz lifts her hair back from her face and tucks it behind her ear, and begins to recount the events of last night.

My mother hides her mouth behind her bony hands. What can she do? How can she help me? Which door should she knock upon? Should she go to her cousin who's become a high-ranking official?

No, never! How can she beg for help from someone she was once in love with when she was young—but whom she left for another man? Her cousin has never forgotten my father's jealousy. Every time my father set eyes on my mother's cousin, in his flashy military clothes, his blood would rise. He would say, "Fuck the mother and sister of Taraki and Hafizullah Amin!" He would pick petty political arguments, and my mother's old flame would get upset and walk out. Then my father would crow with joy in my mother's face. The very day my father took another wife and fled to Pakistan, my mother's cousin came to our house with a sheepish look on his face. My mother spat at him and threw him out.

What will my mother do?

She will ask Mahnaz to wait in the front room while she goes to put on her veil.

She will come to see me with Mahnaz.

❖ ❖ ❖

"Look, Father, I'm drawing this for you."

Yahya's little hand moves a crayon across a black sheet of paper.

"What is it?"

"A moth."

"But where is it?"

"You can't see it because it's too dark."

Someone is banging on the door. It must be Mahnaz with my mother. Mahnaz? No, why would she be knocking on her own front door?

Yahya lifts his head out of the night and its creatures. The banging gets louder. Who on earth can it be? Another search party? Yahya's uncle's moaning can be heard along the corridor. Yahya leaves his invisible moth in its eternal night and heads for the corridor. I run after him. The banging gets even louder.

Yahya's uncle stands in the middle of his room, his strangely arched arms wrapped around his scrawny skeleton, his wails increasing in their intensity. Will we have to go back into that hole again? I take his hand. It's shaking. I'm shaking too. The banging still echoes around the courtyard. We reach the end of the corridor. Yahya's uncle continues to moan.

"Don't be scared, Uncle Moheb, it's all right."

But Uncle Moheb will not be reassured.

"Uncle Moheb, look, my father is here," says Yahya, taking his other hand. "There's no need to be frightened!"

Moheb wails even more bitterly. I drop his hand. The banging continues relentlessly.

"Uncle Moheb, it's only my mother. She's forgotten the key. I'll go and let her in."

Moheb calms down. His gaze, as always, set in the middle distance. Holding him by the hand, Yahya leads his distorted frame back into his room and sits him down on a cushion. And there we abandon him.

Once we're back in the corridor, the banging stops. Whoever it was has gone.

"I think it was my grandma . . ."

Yahya is tempted to go outside.

"No, Yahya! Your mother told you not to open the door to anyone."

"Not even to my granny?"

"But it might not have been your grandma."

Looking puzzled, Yahya goes back to his uncle, and I return to my place in the room.

Yahya's moth is completely invisible against paper that's the color of the night. I find a piece of white chalk in his pencil case and draw a moth for him.

But why should this moth be visible?

I scribble over the moth with a pencil the exact shade of the paper: night.

I got off the bus outside the university to find Enayat waiting for me in the entrance. He asked me if I'd like to go for a drink. We went off to the tomb of Sayed Jamaluddin. A few couples were declaring their love in the hidden depths of the shrubbery. Propped up against the marble tomb, we drank some wine and talked about our lives.

We'd only been there a while when Enayat's sister turned up—sobbing, utterly distraught—bearing the terrible news that their brother had committed suicide in prison. Enayat smashed the bottle of wine against Sayed Jamal-Udin's sepulchre and immediately ran off home. I made my way back to my class.

A few days before the Revolution Day celebrations, a decree was issued ordering everyone in Kabul to either paint their front door red or hang a red flag from the window. Enayat's brother and his friends went to the abattoir, anointed some sheets with sheep's blood, and then sold them to their neighbors. By Revolution Day, the blood had turned black. Enayat's brother and his friends were slung in jail.

I walk into the lecture theater. Above the huge blackboard they've rigged up a red banner on which a famous slogan has been written in white:

> If I do not stand up,
> If you do not stand up,
> If he does not stand up,
> Then who will light a torch in the midst
>   of this darkness?

If Enayat's brother hadn't killed himself, maybe he'd have turned out like Yahya's uncle. A young man with no youth. With no soul. A body suspended between two arches. I do not want to see what Enayat's brother and Yahya's uncle have seen. No! I do not want my mother to put her breast in my dry mouth for me to suck her blood; or like Enayat's mother, to cry over her own son's empty grave . . . I want to stay alive.

"My mother's here!"

Yahya runs to the door. Once the door opens the house is filled with the smell of Mahnaz—and my mother too! I hurtle down the passageway. An old woman walks into the courtyard behind Mahnaz. But she is not my mother. Mahnaz doesn't close the street door. She stands completely still, as if she wants the old woman to finish what she has to say and leave as quickly as possible.

"Grandma!"

Yahya tries to run out to the courtyard, but I hold him back.

"Yahya, your granny mustn't see me!"

He stares at me with complete bewilderment. We fall silent. He drops his question, and his little head.

❖ ❖ ❖

"One day grandmother said that you had died in Pul-e-Charkhi . . . but she can't say that anymore, can she, if she sees you're alive?"

"But, Yahya, I'm not really your . . ."

No, I can't bring myself to say it.

"When I told her that you came to see me in my dreams and one day I would catch you, she laughed in my face and got cross with me . . . But if she sees you now . . ."

"I'll go and tell her I'm back myself. Now, go and see how your uncle is doing . . ."

With a heavy heart, the child returns to Moheb's room. The old woman has come nearly as far as the terrace. Stealthily, on tiptoe, I creep back to the room. Through the open window I can hear Mahnaz's mother-in-law say, "You can do what you want, but I'm taking Yahya with me. I'm not leaving my grandson in the care of a madwoman!"

I lift a corner of the curtain and peer cautiously outside. Mahnaz is still standing by the open street door. Her face is rigid. She's seething inside. I can't hear what she's saying, but I can guess. She pronounces the words very slowly, as if she were doling them out. Her mother-in-law sits on the steps up to the terrace. Her shaking voice echoes again:

". . . Anwar will show you we have not yet completely lost our honor!"

As she makes her reply, Mahnaz points toward the door. Silenced and exhausted, her mother-in-law drags herself up from the steps, adjusts her veil, and heads for the street. Her voice echoes through the front yard of her dead son:

"So now you're so important, you have the audacity to throw me out of my own son's house! Mark my words, you'll regret . . ."

Her voice follows her bent old body and disappears into the street. Mahnaz closes the door firmly behind her, and turns toward the house. I wait in the corridor. Yahya too.

The child opens the door to his mother. Like Yahya, I want to throw myself in Mahnaz's arms. She smells of my mother. My heart pounds. My hands shake. My tongue manages, "Hello . . . how are you?"

Mahnaz takes off her shoes that have kicked up the living room carpet. This time she doesn't tuck away the hair that has fallen in front of her eyes. With lowered gaze she draws her little son's head into her arms.

Why won't she look at me?

"I found your house. They're all fine. I saw your mother. I told her everything. Thank God you didn't go there. At prayer time this morning, they searched the house. They were looking for pamphlets. They said you were out distributing leaflets last night . . ."

"That's not true! Believe me . . ."

"It's OK, I know . . ."

"How's my mother?"

"Everyone is fine. But anxious."

"Why didn't my mother come back with you?"

"She wanted to come, but I wouldn't let her."

Why not, I wonder. Mahnaz tells Yahya to go to his room. She answers my unspoken question:

"Your house may well be under surveillance. Your mother's coming here would be incredibly dangerous. Meanwhile, she's trying to come up with a plan to get you out of this mess. She wants you to leave Kabul as soon as you can. She'll come over later this afternoon. I've told her where we live."

Her eyes, hidden by her hair, still avoid mine.

What else is she hiding?

She leaves. In the privacy of her room, she lifts the weight of my questioning gaze from her worn-out body, and sits down.

All at once, the scent of my mother evaporates from the corridor.

If I didn't exist, I wouldn't be here.

If I wasn't here, Mahnaz would cry her eyes out; she would go wild with grief. Instead, she pens in her tears and her fury. Instead, she immolates her anguish in a pit at the bottom of her heart, until she's alone again.

Just like my mother. Only once did I ever see her cry—on the day my father took another wife. My mother appealed to my uncle—her brother—who was close to my father. My uncle laughed in her face. He sided with my father. My mother sobbed and wailed. And then my grand-father gave her a little talisman, something Da Mullah Saed Mustafa had given him a long time ago. From that day on, whenever my mother felt her fury rise, she put the talisman between her teeth and bit down on it as hard as she could. Clamped down on her gag, my mother's twisted mouth would not let out a cry. Her eyes lit up with fear, she'd make herself busy with menial tasks in the kitchen. Sometimes, she'd even rewash the dishes. After a while, she'd perform her ablutions and say a prayer of atonement.

I never understood what it was exactly that she needed to purge: anger or hate? Pride or humiliation?

My mother would say that all the water in the world had sprung from her tears.

"Have some grapes, Father!"

Yahya, bearing a bunch of grapes, has slipped in quietly; he crosses his legs and sits down next to me. I pull myself up on the cushion.

"Where's your mother?"

"In the kitchen."

I take a grape from the bunch and drop it into my mouth. Yahya holds the grapes up in front of me like an offering.

I wonder whether Mahnaz told her mother-in-law anything about me that could have made her angry and fear for her honor.

I stand up.

"Honor": what an honorless word it is!

I must talk to Mahnaz. Why has she gone to so much trouble, and fought with her mother-in-law, for my sake? Why does she want to protect me, no matter what the cost?

Maybe she won't protect me. Maybe this is all a trap. She wants something from me. But what? Am I stuck here? Why would she want to keep a strange man hidden in her house? So we can have an affair on the sly? After all, she's certainly very intimate with her brother. She puts her breast in his mouth . . .

No. I can't stay here a minute longer! I move toward the corridor. Clasping the bunch of grapes, Yahya stares at my clumsiness.

How could I think of Mahnaz like that! Why can't I believe that a woman could rescue a strange man without any ulterior motive? Maybe rescuing me is an attempt to redress the balance since she couldn't save her husband. Maybe by helping me, she'll reclaim her dignity.

I sit down on the cushion again.

For the sake of Mahnaz and her secret, I've abandoned my mother—left her walled up alone with her fears all night long; I've condemned Parwaneh to stare from her window, hopelessly, for hours on end; I've left Farid, dejected, waiting outside my bedroom door . . .

I take the bunch of grapes from Yahya.

The mystery of Mahnaz is hidden in the lock of hair that she keeps having to tuck behind her ear.

I give myself up to the lifeless flowers on the cushion.

❖ ❖ ❖

I've never felt this close to a woman before apart from my mother and Parwaneh. I've never been part of another woman's life. No other woman has ever entered my consciousness like this. In the space of just one night, I have gone through a thousand different emotions with this woman, as though something momentous has happened between us. She has given me shelter. My life is in her hands. It is hers.

Yahya picks grapes off the bunch I hold in my hands.

"Dear Mahnaz, why do you want to help me?"

She'll shrug her shoulders. She won't say a word. She'll give me a look that says, "What a stupid question! If you don't want to be here—leave! Go on—God be with you!"

"I'm asking you because I need to know what's going on—and I need to get to know you, too . . ."

"Why?"

"In your eyes, in the things you say, there's a secret that I see in my mother's eyes . . . a secret I've never . . ."

With two fingers she'll lift the hair from the side of her face and she'll laugh at me! She'll smile at me and shake her head. She'll assume I'm trying to catch her out . . . that it's impossible for me to believe a woman can have integrity . . . that . . .

"Farhad, I'm so sorry to have left you on your own all this time!"

Her voice shocks me from my reverie. I try to sit up on the cushion, then I stand up, clutching the stripped bunch of grapes that I pass, stupidly, from one hand to another. I feel sure that Mahnaz has been waiting outside the door reading my mind, hearing every word of our imaginary conversation. I turn scarlet with shame.

"I'm making something to eat."

With unsteady steps, I cross the carpet toward her. Without having a clue of what I'm about to say to her, I hear myself speak:

"My mother . . . Please don't go to any more trouble . . . She'll come as . . . soon as possible . . ."

"Of course, but in the meantime, let's have something to eat."

She stares at the naked bunch of grapes I'm holding in my hands. I move a little closer to her. My heart pounds in my chest.

"I've caused you so much trouble . . . I hope that . . . Yahya's grandmother . . ."

A grim smile settles on her lips.

"Don't worry about that."

She looks away from the shriveled branch in my hands and peers down the corridor.

"As I told you last night, my husband was murdered when he was in prison . . ."

"Peace be with him . . ." I say, softly.

"And now my husband's family wants me to marry my brother-in-law . . . But that's not what I want . . . I keep telling them I don't feel as though I'm really a widow. No one has seen my husband's body . . . since, in prison, they bury the dead in unmarked, communal graves . . ."

A sudden shiver goes right through me. I don't know whether it's a tremor of fear, or hatred, or anger—or from thinking thoughts like these about Mahnaz. I look down, away from her face, and stare at the carpet.

"Now all of my husband's family is going to Pakistan . . . But I don't want to go . . ."

Mahnaz's delicate feet blend into the black patterns on the carpet. The patterns have neither ending nor beginning. These elaborate octagonal designs are infinitely intertwined and interwoven with endless other octagons. The octagons give birth to rectangles, the rectangles give birth to tiny dots . . .

I snap out of staring at the carpet when I catch sight of Mahnaz's feet moving a little to the left. The lock of hair hides the left side of her face. I look into her eyes. She is waiting for an answer to a question that I have not yet been asked.

The sudden loud hiss of the pressure cooker takes Mahnaz's questioning gaze out of the room.

I stay behind to keep company with her unspoken words.

Why on earth did I keep my mouth shut? Why didn't I say something helpful in response to Mahnaz's terrible story? Maybe this was the first time she'd confided this painful secret to anyone. And all I did was stand there, red-faced and dumbstruck, staring like an idiot at the carpet!

Mahnaz didn't just want to tell me about her suffering. Like any other woman, like my mother, she wanted someone to understand her pain. She wanted to share her distress with somebody else. The last thing she needs is another Moheb in her life—someone deaf to her cries and dead to the world!

I go back to my cushion under the window. Reaching one hand behind the colossus of candle wax, I open the curtains to let more light fall onto the carpet. Below me, the courtyard, alive with anxiety, awaits my mother's arrival.

I collapse with exhaustion onto the flower-patterned cushion.

In the clear light of day, the black lines on the carpet seem blacker than ever, and its deep red background glows with the quintessence of red. Suddenly I realize that these carpets are woven from hatred and anger. Black against red! As though the carpet weavers twisted the red weft of their anger with the black warp of their hatred . . . Women carpet weavers . . . children . . .

I'm sick to death of carpets!

I turn away from the black dots inside the rectangles of the carpet and lean back against the cushion's flowers.

Up on the ceiling, a spider has spun its web around the lampshade.

I lower my face into her hands. Her hands are frozen. They tremble. But they hold me so tenderly!

My mother. She got here an hour ago. In disguise, well concealed—underneath the local laundrywoman's veil. She couldn't risk anyone spotting how scared she was coming here.

At first even I didn't recognize her. There was a knock on the door. From behind the curtain I could see it was a heavily veiled woman. With her was an old porter with a large carpet balanced on one shoulder. They entered the room with Mahnaz. The porter deposited the carpet in the corner and went out. Then Mahnaz left too, closing the door behind her. My mother took off her veil and examined her battered son with exhausted eyes, her troubled face lit up with a beautiful smile. But not a word escaped her lips, shut tight as always between those two tense brackets. And me, I shook. I shook deep down inside. I trembled in her arms. I could not speak. We stand together in silence. My head in her hands. I can hear her breath laboring in her chest. I can't open my eyes. I imagine she has loosened her blouse to take her worn-out breast and place it between my dry lips.

Her hand, shaking with anxiety, hovers over the gash on my temple.

"At three this afternoon, a trafficker is coming here to take you to Pakistan wrapped up in this carpet . . ."

That's all she says. I lift my head from her hands.

"Mother, but . . ."

"But what?"

Looking directly into her terrified eyes, I find that all that I wanted to say is reduced to a single word:

"Nothing."

She hands me an envelope. Inside is my father's address, together with a little money.

"Mother, where should I go?"

"Where else can you go?"

I put my father's unbearable pride back in the envelope.

"But what about you? And Parwaneh? What about Farid?"

She looks away, taking my hand in hers. She clears her throat. Trying not to cry.

"Things will get better soon."

I press her hand to get her to look at me. But she won't. She stares down at the carpet. Perhaps, for the very first time, my mother grasps the hatred and anger that has gone into weaving this carpet.

"Mother, let's both go!"

A bitter laugh shakes her tiny frame. Her eyes repeat her father's words:

"Faith is better than a roof!"

The door opens. It's Mahnaz.

"I've brought you some tea."

She puts the tray down next to my mother and pours out two cups of tea. The brackets round my mother's mouth relax, allowing a smile.

"I can't thank you enough for your kindness . . . I'm so sorry we've caused you such trouble . . ."

Mahnaz hands my mother a cup of tea.

"Here, please have some tea. These days it's important we all take care of each other."

She stands up and leaves the room.

My mother stops staring at the door through which Mahnaz has just walked and turns to look straight into my eyes.

"What a kind woman! After you've left, I'll give her a present."

She soaks a sugar cube in her tea.

"Where is her husband?"

"He was executed."

My mother takes the sugar cube out of her tea and drops it onto the saucer. It melts as quickly as her heart. Her horrified gaze travels out of the room to the corridor, where it alights on my battered shoes.

"May God be with him!"

She mutters something under her breath. Her trembling hands bring the sugarless tea to her anxious lips. She downs it in one gulp. As if she wants to wash the shame from her throat with hot tea. If she were at home, she'd get up and leave the room, she'd hold her hands under the cold tap, then she'd rewash the washed dishes, or rescrub Parwaneh's immaculate school veil . . .

Yahya peeps his head around the door to stare at me and my mother.

"Yahya, come in."

At the sound of my voice, the child steps into the room. But at the sound of his mother, he quickly goes back to Moheb's room.

"She has a child?"

"Yes."

My mother's troubled eyes, looking more lost than ever before, scan the empty corridor anxiously. I dare not tell her that Yahya calls me "Father."

"Mother, how did you find the trafficker?"

"Your uncle found him," she says, her gaze still lost in the corridor.

"How much money does he want?"

"His payment is that carpet. We don't have the money, so it's the only thing I could think of."

"Mother . . . "

She puts the cup back on the tray, drained of tea, filled with sadness.

The way she looks at me makes me lose track of what I want to say. She lifts her sky-blue skirt from the flower-patterned cushion, and stands up.

"I have to go. The laundry-woman is waiting for her veil."

"No, Mother, I can't go without you."

"You must go. I'll bring Parwaneh and Farid with me once I sell the house."

I can hear the doubt in her voice.

She takes up the veil from a corner of the room.

"I've forgotten how to put it on!"

She laughs a small, bitter laugh. A laugh that makes me shiver. She adjusts the veil over her hair. The brackets around her mouth shake.

"Mother, I'm coming with you."

She covers her face, as though she hasn't heard what I said.

"Mother, I can't just leave without seeing Farid and Parwaneh . . ."

She brings her grief-stricken hands out from under her veil and presses them against my heart. My voice fails. My eyes fill with tears. I put my face in her hands. My mother's broken voice emerges from behind the folds of her veil:

"May God watch over you . . ."

Why does she move away? Isn't she going to kiss me goodbye? I need to look into her eyes again, I need to see the brackets that muffle her cries. I stumble toward her. I reach out to touch the veil that is covering her eyes but I cannot feel the exhausted face it hides. The veil is wet. My mother is crying. Crying without a sound. She is crying between those two brackets. She is crying under her veil. My mother is rinsing the laundry-woman's veil with her tears.

She takes another step away. Her whole body is shaking under her veil. She moves into the corridor. She searches for her shoes. I stand there, lost, like a button dropped on the black and red patterns of the carpet. Yahya and Mahnaz come out of Moheb's room. My legs won't move. Without a look, without a smile, my mother says to Mahnaz, "God be with you . . . May God reward . . ."

Her words are swallowed by her veil. My feet have been sewn to the carpet by the threads of hatred and anger that were woven together by all those nameless women and children. My mother is gone.

My feet are sewn to the carpet.

My heart breaks at the sound of the door to the terrace closing behind her.

"Mother . . ."
My voice breaks.

The carpet is sewn to my feet.

"Mother . . ."

I am nothing but a pattern in a carpet.

"Father!"

...?!

"Father!"

Everything has gone black.

I have passed out on the carpet. When I come to, Yahya is sitting down next to me.

My mother is gone. She has left with my last sight of her hidden away under her veil.

Yahya hands me a glass of water. I disentangle myself from the patterns on the carpet and answer Yahya's kind look with a smile. In agony, I haul myself up again onto the cushion under the windowsill. I drink the water that Yahya has brought for me.

"Where's your mother?"

"In the kitchen."

I get up. The smell of onions leads me to the kitchen. With her back to the door, Mahnaz is busy slicing them into rings. For a moment, standing by the door, I watch her in silence. What am I doing here? Why am I shaking?

❖ ❖ ❖

Mahnaz senses my presence. She turns toward me. With the end of her sleeve she wipes the onion-tears from her eyes, and smiles at me. This is the very first time I've seen her smile. She smiles to make me understand that her tears have been caused by onions, not by grief. I try to smile back. I manage a hopeless parody of a smile.

Mahnaz slides the onions into a saucepan. As always, the smell of frying onions makes me hungry. The kitchen fills with the aroma of my mother's cooking. As always, my heart beats faster. I want to take a piece of bread and steal some of the fried onions from the pan. I want to put my hands on Mahnaz's shoulders. I want to tuck that lock of hair behind her ear myself.

"You must be hungry."

"The smell of frying onions always makes me hungry."

I lean against the door. I find myself imagining I've lived in this house for years, that I've known Mahnaz for years, that Yahya has called me "Father" for years, that my mother has visited us here for years. For years I've wanted to go away, but I haven't been able to. For years I've been asking her the same question:

"Why don't you come away with me?"

Mahnaz stops stirring the onions. My heart thumps. She turns to smile at me. A bitter smile.

"Dear Farhad, life is not that simple!"

She turns back to the pan. The smell of frying onions makes the house seem more homely.

"If I go to Pakistan, I'll have to marry my brother-in-law."

I stop leaning on the door and move over to the wall.

"But where is *your* family?" I ask her.

She pours boiling water into the pan, and her voice comes from the middle of a cloud of steam.

"Only my brother Moheb is left with me. The rest have gone to Germany."

She stirs the onions with a wooden spoon.

"I've not been in touch with them for years."

She takes a deep breath.

"When I was born . . ."

She places the lid on the pan.

". . . I didn't scream, I didn't smile, I didn't cry . . ."

She takes a few chicken wings out of a bag.

". . . They all thought I'd been born deaf and dumb. So when I was a little girl they arranged for me to be married to my cousin. He was deaf and dumb too. When I got older, though, it turned out that I was neither deaf nor dumb. But by then it made no difference to them . . ."

She washes the chicken wings under the tap.

". . . My father died when I was young. I was never close to my mother. When I grew up, I had no choice but to marry my cousin. So I ran away and married Yahya's father."

She lifts the lid and pours some more water in the pan.

"The night when all of my family fled to Pakistan, my mother came and left Moheb behind on our doorstep."

With my back to the wall I slide down slowly until I'm crouching on the floor. Once again, the story of Mahnaz's life reduces me to silence. Once again, anything I could say seems completely pointless.

I forget the smell of frying onions. For some time, I stare at the black locks of her hair falling down her back.

"Is there anything I can do to help you?" I ask her without thinking.

She gives me a painful smile.

"Nothing!"

Even her throwaway "Nothing" bears the weight of a history that demands to be known.

"Why don't we go to Iran? Your husband's family couldn't find you there."

She remains silent for a moment. Tipping the chicken wings into the pan, without turning around to look at me, she says, "Farhad my dear, my husband's family are very strange people. The type for whom blood and family honor are one and the same. Don't get yourself mixed up with us. I'll be fine here."

She puts the lid back on the saucepan.

In a corner of the kitchen, my heart fills with love.

All of us sit around the tablecloth spread on the floor of Moheb's room. All of us eat in silence. Chicken wings have taken the place of words. As if we had already said all there is to be said. No more questions to be put, no more answers to be heard. We are all waiting for the trafficker to bang on the door.

A knock. Yahya gets up and runs down the corridor, a chicken wing in his hand. The sound of his small feet echoes from the courtyard. He reaches the street door. Having answered the door, he rushes back out of breath.

"It's a man who says he's come to buy a carpet."

I jump to my feet without thinking. My heart plummets. My legs go weak.

"It's the trafficker," I tell Mahnaz, "I can't go with him!"

Mahnaz gets up and tucks her hair behind her ear.

"Put on your shoes," she says in her usual even tone.

I stare deep into her eyes. But she turns her head away. I want to put my life in her hands. Mahnaz leaves the room. Moheb starts to moan. I begin to cry inside, in silence.

Mahnaz takes the trafficker to the room where I spent the night.

"Father, will you come back soon?" Yahya asks, grasping my hand, greasy with chicken.

I follow the trafficker into the room without even washing my hands. He has spread our carpet across the floor. From it rises the sound of all the guests who've ever walked across it. Our best carpet. Its color seems even redder than before, its "elephant-foot" patterns even bigger and blacker.

"Hey, Brother, let's give it a go."

Mahnaz is standing by the door. Yahya leans his little head against the green flowers patterning his mother's skirt. My unsteady frame collapses into the middle of the carpet under Mahnaz's inscrutable gaze. The trafficker swiftly rolls me up into the carpet saying "Ya Ali!" as he heaves us both up onto his strong, broad shoulders and takes a first step. From the sound of his feet I can work out when we leave the room and when we reach the courtyard. Where is he going? Where is he taking me? No, first I have to say goodbye to Mahnaz! The street door is opening. No!

"Mahnaz!"

My cry is smothered in the patterns of our carpet. I try to struggle free.

"Brother, be quiet! We're outside in the street."

"I don't want to go! Hey, do you hear me? Mahnaz! Yahya!"

My cries are cut off by the sound of a car door opening. The trafficker brings the carpet down from his shoulders and slides it inside. He shuts the door. I want to move, I want to get free of these carpet patterns.

"Father! Father!"

Yahya's cries chase the sounds of our guests from this carpet forever.

I have no idea anymore whether the patterns on our carpet have gotten bigger, or whether I've gotten smaller. I'm running along the black lines of the patterns. My father stands over me. He is big. Immense. He won't allow my feet to slip off the black patterns onto the red background of the carpet. I'm running. I'm spinning. As if I am trapped in a labyrinth. The black patterns have neither beginning nor end. All the lines turn back on themselves. Octagons and rectangles. I am crying and running.

"Run! Run!" my father shouts. "Shut up and stop crying! You unbeliever!"

I'm trying to work out how to escape from these octagons and rectangles without stepping onto the red background. The only possible way is to get through to the other side, to run and run till the carpet wears out under my feet. I run. I'm getting smaller and smaller with every turn. I run and I run. The patterns get bigger and bigger. As though I'm a part of the carpet's design. I can feel the texture of the threads.

I only know I'm in the carpet because of its smell. I can't see a thing. Just blackness. I can't breathe. I can't move.

"Tell him to keep still . . ."

I make out the sound of the trafficker's voice over the monotonous thrum of the engine.

"Brother, keep still," I hear a woman say. "We're coming up to a checkpoint."

I hold in my breath and my fear under the weight of the two bodies that sit on top of the carpet.

My head spins in the red-and-black labyrinth of the carpet.

As usual he sits with his hands laced across his bloated stomach, a look of complete indifference on his face.

"Hello, Father!"

No, I will not call him Father.

"Hello."

"Hello."

What next?

"So, what brings you here, then?"

Hiding his contempt with a laugh.

"You left your mother, your sister, and your brother behind to come and visit me?"

His arrogant sneer brings back the memory of the last thing I said to him before he walked out on us with his second wife in tow—a phrase that unfortunately escapes my mind as two people shift about on the carpet wrapped around me. The car comes to a halt. I leave my father with his disdain, his fat stomach, and his second wife. The back door of the car opens.

"Where are you going?" booms a voice.

The voice of the trafficker replies to the soldier: "Moosa-e-Logar."

"Who are these people?"

"My two wives."

I can feel the bayonet of a gun poking the carpet.

"Where are you taking this carpet?"

"It's a wedding present for my brother."

The door slams shut. The car moves off. The two people get off the carpet. A cold sweat films my entire body. They loosen the two pieces of cloth tucked into the ends of the carpet. I gasp for air.

My sweating face trapped inside the carpet heightens its smell. Such a familiar smell. The smell of our front room. Parwaneh used to play marbles on the black patterns of this carpet. Farid used to race his matchbox cars along its black lines . . . It was the best carpet in the house—my mother's dowry, given by her father to take to her new husband's house.

No. I will never go to see my father. I can't possibly stay in Peshawar. I'll go to Islamabad. But I don't really like it there either. I'll have to go somewhere else. Karachi or Lahore. I'll get through this somehow or other. Soon I'll be able to send for my mother, Parwaneh, and Farid.

I scratch my face on my mother's dowry.

The car stops. The carpet with me wrapped up inside it is hauled out of the car and put on the ground. I roll over as it's unrolled. The half-light of dusk hurts my eyes. I fill my chest with fresh air and the smell of the countryside. The trafficker drags my stiff frame free of the black patterns of the carpet. The car has pulled over by the side of a dirt track on top of a hill covered with thorn bushes.

"We're taking a shortcut. We'll be in the village in under an hour."

The trafficker takes a packet of cigarettes from his waist-coat pocket and offers me one.

"Thanks, but I don't smoke."

Putting a cigarette between his lips, he lights up. Then he squats down on the carpet. Covered by their veils, his two wives leave the car to sit on the opposite corner of the carpet, turning their backs to us. I stand up.

The cigarette smoke and the trafficker's voice steal over the golden slope of the hill.

"All being well, we'll set off for Pakistan at dawn the day after tomorrow, by morning prayers. It'll take two days. You . . ."

The low laughter of his two wives rises above his words.

"What are you laughing about?"

Both women immediately fall silent.

"You'll stay in the village mosque," the trafficker goes on. "But you mustn't talk to a soul. By the way, do you have a student card?"

"No."

"An ID card?"

"No, the soldiers took them off me."

"Never mind. Do you have any papers at all?"

I go through my pockets mechanically. Other than two thousand Afghanis and a folded paper with my father's address written on it, there's nothing else.

My heart gives a sudden leap. Of happiness. Happiness about what? Mahnaz must have looked for my ID card and student card in the sewer . . . and found them . . . and my clothes . . . Will she hang on to them?

"Hey, Brother, snap out of it!"

I come back to the hill and our carpet, which is spread over the ground. On one corner sits the trafficker wearing his astrakhan hat. On the other, the two women with their blue and yellow veils . . . The setting sun merges their shadows with the carpet's black patterns.

"Sorry, what did you say?"

"Do you know how to pray?"

"I think so, roughly . . ."

"Some nights the religious students get together and sleep in the mosque. They ask lots of questions of students like you from Kabul. But don't worry. You'll be all right unless you get into any kind of political discussions with them . . . It's not a good idea to let on that you've been to university . . . Tell them instead that you left school after sixth grade and then got a job."

I wonder if Mahnaz has washed my clothes? Will she give them to Moheb? No.

"Do you know anyone in Pakistan?"

"No."

He says nothing. His narrow eyes, hidden under his thick eyebrows, follow the smoke curling from his cigarette into the fading light.

"Don't you even have an address?"

"Is it important?"

"Yes. If anyone asks you, tell them you've already sent your wife and child to Pakistan and that they're all there waiting for you."

"My father is in Pakistan."

"Then why did you say you didn't know anyone there?"

"I don't want to have anything to do with my father."

"OK, that's up to you. But it's a good idea to have an address."

No. I have no desire whatsoever to be beholden to my father.

"Why didn't you bring your wife and child along with you?"

"My wife and child?"

Mahnaz and Yahya!

"It would be much easier if you were with your family."

He throws away his cigarette butt. His voice is clear in the still evening air.

"Ya, Allah! Let's go."

The two women get off the carpet and head toward the car. The trafficker rolls up the carpet, empty of me, and tosses it into the back of the car. I get in too. The backseats of the car have been taken out. I sit on the rolled-up carpet. The women settle themselves in the front seat next to their husband.

Traveling downhill, the car kicks up a thick cloud of dust as it speeds around the bends in the road. The last red seconds of the day burnish the shoulders of the trafficker as he drives.

I ease myself off the carpet onto the metal floor of the car. I put my head on the carpet and kiss my mother's footprints.

Once she'd left Mahnaz's house, safely hidden under her veil, my mother went to the Shah-Do-Shamsira Mosque. There she tied a ribbon to the grill of the shrine and made a prayer for her son to get to Pakistan safely. My mother wept. But no one saw her tears. No one asked, "Mother, why are you crying?"

My mother wept to herself, lonelier than ever before. Walking back home from the shrine, she concealed her terrified face beneath her veil. More anonymous than ever before. More insignificant than ever before. Unable to confide to a soul, "My oldest son, the man of my house, has become a fugitive!"

And no one replied, "Mother, may his absence be filled with patience and grace."

Shrouded in her veil, crazy with grief, my mother shed her tears in the backstreets of the ignorant city before finally reaching our home. She wrapped up her distress in the veil and gave it back to the laundry-woman. She squirreled herself away in the safety of her kitchen to rewash the clean dishes. When the laundry-woman left, she took all the clean linen off the clothesline and washed it all again.

She hasn't said a word to Parwaneh or Farid about my escape. She'll tell them tomorrow. My mother always hangs on to bad news. She lives with it for a while, she weeps, she curses . . . and then, the next day, during breakfast, she'll announce, "Children, Farhad has gone to Pakistan."

Parwaneh rushes next door to take out her fury by sinking her teeth into her pristine school veil. Farid, with tears in his eyes, stays close to my mother. His childhood is over. His chest swells. Now he is the man of the house. He takes the worn-out hands of my mother in his own small grasp and presses them tenderly. Tomorrow they will move the green kilim from my room and lay it on the floor of the front room.

The car comes to a halt next to a small mud compound. The trafficker unloads the atmosphere of our house, rolled up in our carpet, and, along with his two wives, takes it into the compound.

I stay behind with two earless dogs that appear from nowhere to sniff around the car, a car that is emptied of memories and filled with fear.

In a corner of the mosque a man lies asleep next to me, his head resting on a brick for a pillow. A dervish. A long white beard covers his face. A cloak is spread out over his curled-up body. He's sound asleep. So soundly even the call to prayer hasn't broken into his dreams. He's been left in peace, as if he didn't exist.

Four groups of men sit around four oil-lamps: young and old, faces concealed by lengthy beards. Here, everyone is armed. Alone and unarmed in my corner, I sit with my back propped against the wall of the mosque.

Yahya has sprinkled water on the floor of the terrace, and the smell of dust and worn Hessian matting drifts across the small front yard. Mahnaz has brought Moheb out onto the terrace. Seated around the lantern, the three of them eat together. They eat in silence. What are they thinking about? Are they thinking about me?

"Has Father gone back to the city of Pul-e-Charkhi?" Yahya will ask.

Will Mahnaz tell him that I'm not his father? Perhaps, like me, she won't want to shatter his dreams.

She has hung my freshly washed clothes out to dry on the washing line by the terrace. Mahnaz is thinking of me.

Clouds of hashish smoke permeate the mosque with their pungent smell.

No, Mahnaz won't be thinking of me. She'll do everything in her power to forget all about me. She'll expunge from her life every last sign of me. Once she's washed my clothes, she'll donate them to the poor. I only wish that Mahnaz could know that someone is thinking about her at this very minute—someone who's fallen hopelessly in love with the troublesome lock of hair that insists on hiding one side of her face; someone who's in love with the persistence of her two slim fingers that repeatedly grant asylum to that strand of hair as, once again, they carefully rescue it and tuck it behind her ear . . .

The five bearded young men sitting in the circle closest to me pass their spliff from hand to hand. One of them offers me a drag. But the guy sitting next to him says, without looking at me, "He's from Kabul. He drinks vodka."

The scornful laughter of the little group echoes through the smoke-filled mosque.

I've never once smoked a cigarette in my life, let alone had a spliff.

But what will they think of me if I don't smoke with them? Perhaps they're just testing me. No one's allowed to smoke in a mosque in the first place!

"Just ignore us," says the guy with the black beard who offered me the spliff. "We merely smoke the humble herb of the ignorant poor!"

Hash fumes and mocking laughter spiral above my head. Someone in another group calls out, "*From the ranks encircled of noble men: he who resists . . .*"

The others cry together:

"*Cannot persist!*"

The cacophony in the mosque wakes up the old man who's been sleeping on a brick. Perhaps he's been awake the whole time with his eyes shut. He casts a glance at me. Light from a lantern hanging on a wooden pillar shines in his eyes. He smiles at me—why, I have no idea. Without thinking, I stretch my hand out to take the spliff and put it between my chapped lips. I try to inhale as much smoke as I can. An agonizing fit of coughing tears my chest apart.

"Vodka has mashed up your liver. Hash will mash up your lungs!"

My head rings with their sneering laughter. My limbs feel heavy. My mouth is dry. The mosque is thick with smoke.

What on earth made me smoke hash? Am I mad? I feel as though the blood has drained from my veins. My heart is pounding! I need to sit up.

❖ ❖ ❖

Another group passes their spliff over to me:

"This is a Shah-Jahani, try it!"

I take the proffered spliff. Once more I draw the smoke deep into my lungs. Once more I'm wracked with a coughing fit, making my ribs feel as though they're being dislocated one by one with every explosion.

The dervish raises his head. His eyes are bloodshot. His eyebrows look like two arches tacked to his wrinkled forehead. His jowls have caved in, as though he's sucked his cheeks behind his teeth. He looks both stern and kindly. He moves his lips. He murmurs something under his breath that only he can understand. He throws back the cloak that has covered his wizened frame.

The door of the mosque swings wide open. A man with a white beard appears; he strides inside, bringing with him the absolute silence and weight of the night. Everyone stands up at once and salutes him.

I'm in no fit state to stand up. My head is spinning. I force myself to sit upright by levering my back against the wall.

The man's right eye is hidden under a fold of his black turban. He stands at the front of the mosque. A few of the young men go over to sit by him. The man pulls out an old book from under his arm. He first recites a verse from the Koran himself and then he orders a young man to recite the sura of Joseph.

الرتلک آیات اللکتاب المبین... اد قال یوسف لابیه...

Is it me shaking or the wall of the mosque? I shut my eyes.

"... *Joseph said to his father: O Father, I dreamt that the sun, the moon, and eleven stars prostrated themselves before me.*"

"Praise be to Allah!"

My head is spinning wildly. I finally manage to stand up by hanging on to one of the wooden pillars that's holding up the roof. I leave Joseph with his father and walk toward the door of the mosque.

"*. . . In the tale of Joseph and his brothers can be found many signs of divine wisdom to aid those in search of truth . . .*"

Where have my shoes gone? I step outside in bare feet. It's freezing. The poisonous envy of Joseph's brothers echoes from the mosque and is taken up by the wind. I find myself standing by a stream. The gentle babbling of the water washes the clamor of Jacob's flock from my mind. The sky is clouded over. The moon and the stars lie prostrated at Joseph's feet. I plunge my face into the starless water. The stream cleanses the thick fumes of hash from my lungs and my brain. I drink some water, then walk over to a big tree to have a piss.

Joseph's cries resound inside the mosque. His envious brothers have thrown him into a well. My grandfather's sobs emerge from the darkness. He would weep like Jacob every time he heard that verse.

I aim my piss at the roots of the tree. A bullet whizzes right past me.
    "You atheist infidel!"
    The bullet has lodged in the tree. My piss has come to an immediate halt. The man crashes toward me through the darkness of the night.

"Damn your father! Infidel! What do you think you're doing pissing there like a donkey?"

He waves the barrel of the gun in the direction of the mosque, so I turn and walk back. When we reach the door he shouts, "Stay out! You'll defile the mosque with your filth!"

He goes inside. The trials of Joseph stream through the opened door of the mosque accompanied by a dazzling shaft of lamplight. A passing caravan rescues Joseph from the well, then sells him as a slave to a minister of the Pharaoh.

The man reappears and gestures with his gun for me to follow him. We walk back down to the stream.

"Make your ablutions!"

Mechanically I sit down by the water and begin to wash my hands, then my feet. I repeat the ritual prayer of ablution in silence to myself. My mind is fixed on the barrel of his gun.

"You atheist pig! Infidel! Aren't you going to wash your private parts?"

I am shaking. I don't know whether it's from cold or fear. I pull down my trousers. Just as I begin to wash myself, the man lunges at my balls. I spin backwards.

"Don't you dare move! Why haven't you shaved yourself?"

He grabs at my pubic hair, ripping out a tuft. My yelp skims across the stream.

"You filthy infidel!"

I finish my ablutions and pull up my sopping trousers. I am speechless with fear and humiliation.

He forces me to bend over the stream and begin my ablutions again. Then, in bare feet, under pain of death, I follow the man back to the mosque. I wonder where Joseph has gotten to?

"... *Zulaikha, Potiphar's wife, desired Joseph. She invited him into her chamber and, locking the door demanded, 'Come close to me!'*"

The mosque is alive with the devilish temptations of Zulaikha.

"... *With Joseph intent on escape and Zulaikha intent on holding him fast, they both ran toward the door when suddenly Zulaikha's husband appeared. She cried out to Potiphar: Tell me how you will punish one who wishes to bring harm to your household? Does this crime not merit imprisonment or torture?*"

At the very moment I walk into the mosque, Joseph is thrown into jail. The man sitting at the front signals to the young student to stop reading, consigning Joseph's fate to the depths of the Koran.

The dervish is still in the same place, his eyes glued to a lantern hanging on the wall. The man who has brought me back to the mosque orders me over to the corner. I go to sit near the dervish.

The cleric's voice sounds out from the front of the mosque:

"Consider the plight of Joseph. Consider how Satan set many traps in his path. Never forget that women are the temptation of the devil!"

The man who stopped me from pissing goes over to the cleric and whispers something in his ear. The cleric fixes me with a horrified look and gets to his feet. The crowd of students begin to chant, "Praise be to Allah! Mohammed is our savior!"

But all I can hear is the voice of the dervish:

"Why can't you find in yourself the strength you attribute to Mohammed? In the end, only you can save yourself . . ."

Why don't they finish the story of Joseph? Is my fate really more important than his?

After a brief discussion with two or three of his students, the cleric walks toward me.

"This man is an infidel!" he informs the young bearded man, his eyes burning with hatred. "He must never be allowed to leave for Pakistan to spread his filth."

He turns his back and leaves the mosque.
The dervish settles his head back onto his brick.

The mosque, now emptied of hash fumes, is feverish with Joseph's anxiety.

Joseph lies in chains in a dungeon. In his grief-filled house, Jacob has gone blind. And Joseph's mother? Where is she? Surely her suffering is much worse than Jacob's. And Zulaikha's anguish is even more intense. If Jacob has shut himself away in his room to grieve, these two women have turned themselves into rooms of grief. Not rooms built of bricks and mortar, but rooms carved from the heart! Why does no one ever think about these two stricken women? It is his mother who most needs the healing sight of Joseph's coat of many colors, not his father!

The mosque slumbers in the stupor of hashish. While I take my rest in the strength of Zulaikha's love.

"Unless sleep is less restless than wakefulness, do not rest!"
    It's the dervish standing right above my head. He gives me his hand and leads me out of the mosque.

The mosque, mute and immobile, is soon lost in the mists of the night. We find ourselves, the dervish and I, by the side of the stream. The dervish splashes a little water on my face.

"Who are you?" I ask.

He answers with a smile.

"That's a difficult question. Let me think about it for a while . . ."

He gulps down some water. I am waiting for his answer. He chuckles at my impatience.

"They call me 'the bird.'"

Not another word.

We walk together along the banks of the stream. By his side, all my fears and anxieties have gone. After a few meters, the dervish stops.

"You must always keep moving," he says.

He sits down by the stream and plunges his hand in the water.

"Once water stops flowing, it stagnates. Once water stagnates, it poisons the ground. Be like this stream, always in flux!"

"I want to go back."

"We'll all go back one day."

His hand caresses the water.

"No, I want to go back home, to Kabul."

"Here, they want to murder your body. There, they'll murder your soul!"

He takes the brick out from under his cloak and dips it in the stream.

"One day all of us will be like the mud of this brick."

With a smile on his face, he stands up and leaps to the other side of the stream. We walk beside the water. After a few paces the stream disappears underground.

I don't want to go back to the mosque. I want to stay with this man till dawn. Tomorrow I'll ask the trafficker to take me back to Kabul . . .

"Once you find yourself, always keep moving!"

The dervish's words pull me back from the journey to Kabul in my head. His voice becomes indistinguishable from the gurgling of the stream. We have arrived at its source.

"If you meet someone on your journey, grab him by the scruff of the neck and hang on!"

The dervish is getting fainter. The sound of his voice roots me to the spot.

"And if you never meet anyone . . . then hang on to yourself!"

He's going.

"Where?"

He can't hear me. Or he doesn't want to answer. I can't move.

I'm completely paralyzed. The dervish disappears into the night.

"Don't leave me!"

The despair in my voice settles on the water.

The dervish's voice emerges from the darkness.

"Hang on to yourself!"

A halo of smoke marks the place where the dervish was standing a minute ago. The oil-lamps give off a weak light. Even weaker than I am. Everyone is asleep. I want to get up. I feel too heavy. I lean against the wall of the mosque.

"What are you doing?"

The sleepy voice of the man on the mat next to mine makes me freeze. Without knowing why, I hear myself asking, "Where is the dervish?"

I find myself pointing toward the place where the dervish used to be. The man lowers his head to his mat, covering his eyes with a corner of his turban. His murmuring voice disappears into the folds of cloth.

"What dervish?"

Another voice comes from across the room:

"That weed has really messed his head up!"

"No, he's just talking in his sleep."

They laugh a drowsy, nasty little laugh together. I make a move. The mosque trembles in sympathy. My throat aches with thirst. Water!

I reach the door of the mosque. In the hallway, a young man, his diminutive frame swamped in a huge quilt, opens his sleepy eyes.

"Where are you off to?" he asks.

"I need some water!"

"There's water in that jug."

"It's empty."

"Then go and fill it."

He turns his head away and buries himself in his quilt.

Where's the jug? My body feels entirely drained of both blood and water. I am utterly dry. Dry as the mat under my feet. As though my feet have been sewn to the mat. I can't move my feet. I need some fresh air. The mosque is stifling. There is no air.

"Are you going to say your Nafil prayer?" says the voice under the quilt.

My desiccated body shakes like a leaf. My right foot takes a step. Then stops. Another step. Heavier. Then another. I am outside. With no jug. With no shoes.

Dawn is breaking. The stream babbles loudly. The water invites me toward it. I run. The cold, stony ground shakes beneath my feet. I make it to the stream. Where is the dervish?

I sit down by the side of the stream.

Dawn will reveal where the dervish has gone.

Then the stream goes silent and dries up. I want to get up. My foot slips. I fall into the stream. The stream is a bottomless, dried-up well.

"God Is Great!"

The sound of the call to prayer drags me from the well.

The wolf and the lamb prowl above me in the sky. From the open door of the mosque, yawning voices drift down toward the stream.

I must go back.

Where is the morning star?

I stand up. I move my legs. I must run. I run. On water. On earth.

"STOP!"

Al-Ba'ith!

The voice nails me against the red dawn of the city. Where on earth am I?

My legs shake. I fall to the ground. The metallic taste of blood fills my mouth.

Al-Ba'ith!

A soldier's jackboots, there, right in front of my eyes. Darkness descends.

Is it nighttime?

So soon!

A Thousand Rooms of Dream and Fear is set at a time of acute political upheaval in Afghanistan. In 1973 Mohammed Daoud Khan engineered a coup that overthrew the constitutional monarchy and inaugurated the short-lived Republic of Afghanistan (1973–1978). However, Daoud Khan's rule was marked by corruption and instability and, when the formerly faction-ridden leftist parties overcame their differences to oppose his regime, political chaos and violent state repression ensued.

On April 27, 1978, Hafizullah Amin, the strongman of the Marxist People's Party, organized a coup that toppled Daoud Khan's regime. Amin's mentor, Nur Mohammed Taraki, was installed as party leader, president, and prime minister of the Democratic Republic of Afghanistan, with Amin as his deputy prime minister (until Amin decided he wanted more power and took over the role of prime minister just under a year later). After the April coup many Afghans fled the country. In this novel, Farhad's father is said to have left for Pakistan at that time.

The Soviet Union became increasingly concerned about Amin's burgeoning power and his anti-Islamic stance; the Soviets were convinced that Amin was exacerbating political unrest, particularly in the countryside, and they allegedly advised Taraki to get rid of him. But the attempt to have Amin assassinated was a failure, and instead Amin seized power on September 14, 1979. Taraki was killed in the violence (supposedly smothered to death with a pillow). Although his death was first announced in the *Kabul Times* on October 10, there were conflicting reports of the actual date he was murdered.

Unsurprisingly, Amin's attempts to improve relations with Pakistan and the United States were greeted with alarm by the Soviet Union. Unrest continued to escalate throughout the country, and then on December 24, 1979, Afghanistan was invaded by the Soviet Union. Amin was killed on December 27, and Babrak Karmal was handed the role of president by the invaders.

Though the narrator of *A Thousand Rooms of Dream and Fear* makes few overt references to the political situation in his country, it informs the whole novel. It is also assumed that the reader will understand the powerful social prohibitions that Farhad is breaking by being alone with a woman who no longer has a husband, and that Mahnaz is challenging by allowing her hair to be seen uncovered.

THE TITLE The phrase "a thousand rooms" is a direct translation of a Dari expression that can also mean "labyrinth."

THE EPIGRAPH Shams-e Tabrizi was a thirteenth-century Sufi mystic who was the close companion of the great

Persian poet Mawlana Jalal ad-Din Muhammad Rumi (1207–1273), usually known as Rumi in the West. Shams was responsible for initiating Rumi into Islamic mysticism. After Shams's sudden disappearance in 1248, Rumi's grief and deep devotion to his friend found expression in his *Diwan-e Shams-e Tabrizi* (*The Book of Shams of Tabriz*) in which, as a sign of his love, Rumi attributed his own words to Shams. Poetry, especially that written by Rumi, has the highest possible status and importance for the people of Afghanistan.

BABUR The descendant of Timur (Tamerlane the Great), founder of the Timurid dynasty, Zahiruddin Mohammed Babur (1483–1530) made Kabul the capital of his empire. He was famous for the beautiful gardens and vineyards he planted throughout Kabul, many of which remained until the city descended into chaos during the civil war. After capturing much of present-day Afghanistan, Babur turned his attention to India, where he established the Mughal dynasty. But he never lost his affection for Kabul, and his body is buried there, in Babur's Gardens.

BAGH-E-BALA The summer palace of Abdur Rahman Khan (amir of Afghanistan from 1880 to 1901) was set on a hill to the north of the city, with a magnificent view over Kabul. In 1979 it was a place where young people would go to drink and hang out.

BARZAKH The period between death and final judgment when the fate of the soul remains undecided.

BOOK OF THE DEAD Abu Hamid Muhammad ibn Muhammad al-Ghazali (1058–1111) was one of the greatest Islamic theologians and philosophers of the Middle Ages. He was known in the West as Algazel. A Sufi mystic, his great work, *The Revival of the Religious Sciences*, made Sufism an acceptable part of orthodox Islam. Published in forty volumes, the final part, *On the Remembrance of Death and the Afterlife*, is commonly known as the "Book of the Dead."

DERVISH A Sufi ascetic and mystic. Traditionally, dervishes practice austerity and live a life of poverty and prayer, much like Christian mendicant monks. Like monks, some live in orders and others are solitary. The great Sufi mystic poet Rumi was the founder of the most famous order of dervishes, the Mevlavi, well known for their "whirling" dance, through which they attain ecstasy and spiritual insight.

HAFIZ Mohammed Shams al-Din Hafiz, or Hafiz of Shiraz (1325/6–1389/90) was one of the greatest lyric poets of Persia. A Sufi mystic, he had a profound influence on poetry in Persian and Arabic, especially for his mastery of the *ghazal*. Goethe was very affected by Hafiz's poetry. Hafiz was famous for his poems extolling alcohol as a means of attaining spiritual insight.

HAFT PAIKAR A book written by Nazemi Ghanjavi (c. 1141–1209), who is widely regarded as the greatest romantic epic poet in Persian literature, who introduced colloquial language and a degree of realism to the Persian epic, and whose works form an integral part of the culture of Iran and Afghanistan. *Haft Paikar* (*Seven Portraits*) is the story of the Sassanid king, Bahram-e Gur, who discovers a mysterious room in his palace that contains the portraits of seven beautiful princesses. He goes in search of the princesses, each of whom represents one of the seven virtues.

KALIMA The first verse of the Koran.

KHOSRAW & SHEERIN (see *Haft Paikir*) A book by Nizami Ganjavi. Sheerin (?–628) was the Christian wife of the Persian shah, Khosraw II. She was first immortalized in Persian poetry by Firdausi in his epic, the *Shahnama*. Around 1180, Nizami retold the story, emphasizing Sheerin's love for the master builder, Farhad. Khosraw was so jealous of their love that he tricked Farhad into constructing a tunnel under Mount Beysitoun; he then lied to Farhad, telling him Sheerin was dead, a lie that caused Farhad to fall from the mountain to his death. As a result of Nizami's work, Sheerin and Farhad became symbols of pure, unrequited love. Their plight is recounted in many poems, including Goethe's *West-oestlicher Divan*.

MUNKAR One of the two angels who are assigned to interrogate the dead before judgment day.

NAFIL Practicing Muslims are obliged to pray five times a day. These prayers are called: *Fajr* (at dawn); *Dhuhr* (at midday); *Asr* (in the afternoon); *Maghrib* (at sunset); *Isha* (at night). *Nafil* is the name for an additional, non-obligatory prayer, which can take place at any time.

NAKIR One of the two angels who are assigned to interrogate the dead before judgment day.

NINETY-NINE NAMES OF GOD Also known as the ninety-nine attributes of God (Asma' Allah al-Husná). According to Islamic tradition, Allah has ninety-nine names, each one representing one of his divine qualities. Repeating the names of God is a sacred practice, much as Roman Catholics will recite a litany of the names of saints. In this novel, Farhad recites the names Al-Ba'ith, meaning "the resurrector," Al-Jabbar, meaning "the irresistible, the powerful," and Al-Mumit, meaning "the bringer of death, the destroyer."

PUL-E-CHARKHI Literally, "the bridge that spins around." A large pentagon-shaped prison near Kabul with a fearsome reputation for torture and murder. It was built in the 1970s during the regime of Mohammed Daoud Khan and is still in use today.

SHAH-DO-SHAMSHIRA MOSQUE One of the most important shrines in Kabul, marking the burial sight of an Islamic commander who was said to have fallen in battle against Hindu forces, even though he had continued fighting with a sword in each hand after his head had been cut off.

TOMB OF SAYED JAMALUDDIN A striking landmark on the grounds of Kabul University with huge black marble columns. The campus of Kabul University was built in 1964 with the assistance of the U.S. under Mohammed Daoud Khan.

SARAH MAGUIRE

• • • •

Born in Kabul in 1962, ATIQ RAHIMI was seventeen years old when the Soviet Union invaded Afghanistan. He fled to Pakistan during the war and was granted political asylum in France in 1984. He later enrolled at the Sorbonne and received a doctorate in audio-visual communications. After the fall of the Taliban in 2002, Rahimi returned to Afghanistan, where he filmed an adaptation of his book *Earth and Ashes* (Other Press, 2010). There he has become renowned as a maker of documentary and feature films, and as a writer. The film of *Earth and Ashes* was in the Official Selection at Cannes in 2004 and won several prizes. Since 2002 Rahimi has returned to Afghanistan a number of times to set up the Writers' House in Kabul and offer support and training to young writers and filmmakers. His novel *The Patience Stone* (Other Press, 2010) won the Prix Goncourt in 2008.